HOT & BOTHERED

4

HOT & BOTHERED
4

SHORT SHORT FICTION
ON LESBIAN DESIRE

edited by Karen X. Tulchinsky

ARSENAL
PULP PRESS
Vancouver

ARSENAL PULP PRESS
103 – 1014 Homer Street
Vancouver, BC
Canada V6B 2W9
arsenalpulp.com

The publisher gratefully acknowledges the support of the Canada Council for the Arts and the British Columbia Arts Council for its publishing program, and the Government of Canada through the Book Publishing Industry Development Program for its publishing activities.

Interior design by Solo
Cover design by Val Speidel
Cover photography by Dianne Whelan

Printed and bound in Canada

Tamai Kobayashi's "Jeanie" is from *Quixotic Erotic* (Arsenal Pulp Press, 2003).
Reprinted by permission of the publisher.
Shani Mootoo's "Out on Main Street" is an excerpt from *Out on Main Street* (Press Gang Publishers, 1993).
Reprinted by permission of the publisher.
Lesléa Newman's "The Butch That I Marry" is an excerpt from *Out of the Closet and Nothing to Wear* (Alyson Publications, 1997). Reprinted by permission of the author.
Karen X. Tulchinsky's "Nomi's Phone Call" is an excerpt from *Love and Other Ruins* (Polestar, 2002).
Reprinted by permission of the author.

National Library of Canada
Cataloguing in Publication Data
Main entry under title:
Hot & bothered 4 : short short fiction on lesbian desire / Karen X.
Tulchinsky, editor.
ISBN 1-55152-145-8
1. Lesbians' writings. 2. Lesbians – Fiction. I. Tulchinsky, Karen
X. II. Title: Hot and bothered 4.
PN6120.92.L47H674 2003   808.83'108353   C2003-911208-X

Contents

Acknowledgments

I'd like to thank Brian Lam, Blaine Kyllo, Robert Ballentyne, and Kiran Gill Judge of Arsenal Pulp Press, for editorial support, administrative assistance, marketing and promotions, encouragement, and enthusiasm for the *Hot & Bothered* series. Thanks to Dianne Whelan, once again, for the beautiful cover photo and ongoing friendship. Thanks to Val Speidel for yet another of her gorgeous cover designs, and to Daniel Collins for the author photo. Thanks to my sometime co-editor and all-the-time friend, James Johnstone, for administrative assistance, support, and friendship, and to Richard Banner for his ongoing willingness to bail me out of computer nightmares. Thanks for all the small, independent gay and lesbian, feminist, and alternative bookstores, who against great odds stay in business providing the widest selection of gay and lesbian literature, and thanks to the readers of *Hot & Bothered*: you keep on coming back for more. Thanks to all the contributors in the book for your wonderful stories. Thanks to my friends and family in other cities who have sheltered me while on book tours, including Jess Wells, Tony Speakman, Doug Cooney and Christian Lebano, Lois Fine, Rachel Epstein, Arlene Tully, Lynda Fisher, Dix, Dawn Marie Waddel, Nisa Donnelly, Rachel Pepper, Peter Demas, and Cassandra Nicolaou. Much thanks to Terrie Hamazaki, my lover and fiancée, for loving me, challenging me, and keeping me continually hot and bothered. Thanks always to Charlie Tulchinsky-Hamazaki for unconditional cat love.

For Terrie
still keeping me
Hot & Bothered
and in love

Introduction

What can I say? Sex is popular. This is the fourth in the *Hot & Bothered* series, a collection of short short fiction on lesbian desire. Each time I have put out the call for submissions for the next book in the series, the response from writers has been overwhelming and I have found myself with the enviable task of wading through hundreds of manuscripts on lesbian desire from the United States, Canada, the United Kingdom, Ireland, Australia, New Zealand, and South Africa.

As in the earlier three editions of *Hot & Bothered*, this is not a book of erotica. This is a book on desire. Some stories are graphic, while others are more literary and subtle. The tone of the stories range from humor to heartache, from comedy to drama; they are satirical, sexy, serious, and sweet. Subject matter runs the gamut of lesbian experience: long-term lovers, one-night stands, butch/femme relationships, young love, first love, threesomes, the erotic nature of fruit; sex on vacation, sex on the bus, even sex while tree planting in the wilds of British Columbia. There are stories about grieving, addiction, breaking-up, cultural identity, and sex after a long, dry spell.

There are stories by established, well-known writers, such as Carol Queen, Lesléa Newman, Nisa Donnelly, Barrie Jean Borich, Donna Allegra, Tamai Kobayashi, Wickie Stamps, Sara Graefe, and Shani Mootoo. Emerging writers include Terrie Hamazaki, Gabrielle Glancy, and Suki Lee. And some writers are being published here for the very first time.

Over the past decade, lesbian and gay lives have become increasingly visible in the media, and even though there are more representations of our sex and love lives on film or in television, we still return to literature again and again to discover articulations of who we are.

As an editor, one of my goals has always been to publish anthologies that include voices from many different cultural backgrounds and life experiences. With this fourth book in the popular *Hot & Bothered* series, I invite you to sit back, experience getting bothered, and enjoy getting hot. The pleasure is mine – and yours.

Karen X. Tulchinsky
Vancouver, Canada
September 2003

She's Not a Lesbian

Carol Queen

"I am *not* a lesbian!"

Every time she said this – and she said it quite a bit – her face went all rosy, like a really good sex flush. I knew what her sex flush looked like because she got it just about every time we fucked. Being with her, I developed a new theory: Any woman who says "I am not a lesbian" all the time, probably is.

At home – where she lived with her girlfriend Mary, who was in fact a lesbian, though a deeply closeted one – she said it pretty often. On vacation in San Francisco, she said it even more frequently. She had come to San Francisco with me, not a lesbian but happy to identify that way – I certainly *acted* like a lesbian enough of the time, and I figured that even though I knew I was really bi, with her around, someone needed to say calmly "I am a lesbian" just about as often as she wailed that she wasn't.

In fact, I acted like a lesbian more when she was around than I had in a long time, because meeting her had brought me out of a long drought: arid months of unchosen celibacy interspersed with frantic bouts of juicy masturbation, which, I suppose, temporarily returned my glow but did not address my loneliness and need for love. Perhaps it was one of these glowing days when I met her, or when she decided to make her move. Perhaps, on the other hand, she read the love-hunger and knew I would turn into putty when she touched me. She touched with such assurance that her sexual orientation was never an issue – in fact, she could have been the poster child for Shakespearean provocation. I said this to her often enough:

"Methinks the lady doth protest too much!" I'd crow, and if she got mad it was even more fun, because then I could sniff her fingers and tease her.

"I'm *not* a lesbian!"

And minutes later she'd pull me back into the room borrowed from a friend of a friend and shove me back onto the bed; we set out for Alcatraz countless times that week but never made it all the way to the ferry.

"I'm *not* a lesbian!" But even on the street she'd look both ways and then snake her hand up the leg of my shorts.

"I'm *not* a lesbian!" Yet at the home she and Mary rented with one un-used bedroom, they slept at night under a pile of dogs whose photos they loved to show off. Two rompy dogs – eternally preschool in the park.

This cut close to the reason she knew she wasn't a lesbian: she wanted kids. She fantasized about pretty, rompy kids. Who would the father be? I asked. She named her prettiest male friend – a real flamer, as far as I was concerned.

That didn't seem like a problem. I told her about turkey basters. "You could just buy him the latest issue of *Blue Boy* and wait for him to come over with a jar."

But if it was out of the question to embrace a label that would tell the world how far up my pussy her fingers could go, giving herself to an alter-native reproductive lifestyle was too, too far beyond the pale. She shrieked *really* loudly when I suggested that. Somewhere inside she had a hair-trig-ger meter that she believed would keep her socially safe. She went to old high school friends' weddings. She could not, would not, step across that line of propriety, of identity.

And this would have been a huge problem for me, queer since youth, were it not for the way her fingers felt when they snaked up my shorts. Safe in San Francisco, Miss "I am *not* a Lesbian" would actually slide them right into my always-wet-for-her pussy, right on the street. If she'd been as not-a-lesbian in bed as she was socially, we'd never have gotten anywhere. But there was nothing straight-girl about her, except that soft spot for bridesmaids' dresses.

True, at home I would berate myself after she left my bed, never able to spend the night after sneaking over after work, fucking me silly, then waiting for the first phone call from Mary (which we always let go to the machine): "Is she over there, Carol? Is she with you?" That would be the signal to slow it down or hurry up and come, hurry up and shower, because a few minutes later the phone would ring again: "I know she must be over there . . ." – and then I'd pick up: "Oh, yeah, um, she was just leaving. . . ."

I'd also berate myself, of course, for picking a married girl, though really she picked me and not the other way around. I'd berate myself for hanging out with a closet case, a girlfriend with whom I could never walk down the street hand-in-hand, with whom I could never go dancing without the charade that it was practically her "first time ever dancing with a girl." The worst of both worlds! How could I have found myself so caught up by someone so wrong for me?

And then the phone would ring once more and it'd be her, telling me she was home safe, voice quiet and low and silky, saying she wanted to come back tomorrow.

And then she'd step into my house and the first ten, twenty minutes of kissing would happen on the floor just inside the front door. We'd get to my bed eventually, almost always, but we almost never started out there, because she would push me down right away. We never felt like there was time to climb the stairs first, like two normal people. Whether or not she was a lesbian, we never felt like two normal people, though we came closest in San Francisco.

Mary might have been normal, and all the people around us on the streets. But we were consumed, separated from everyone else by a lust that dared not speak its name. Well, *I* could speak it. And she said it all the time: "I am *not!*"

But you know what they say about actions. She stopped talking when she followed her fingers where they wanted to go.

The Butch That I Marry

Lesléa Newman

"Hey, Flash," I whisper to the prone body lying beside me. "Flash. Flashy. Flash-Flash. Flasheroo. Flashmeister." My beloved is fast asleep and I don't have the heart to wake her, even to say, "Happy Anniversary." It's been eight years since Flash and I became wife and wife, but I remember our wedding like it was yesterday.

Before the wedding came the proposal, of course. We'd only been going out for two months when Flash got down on one knee and asked, "Will you marry me?"

I got up on two elbows, peered over the side of the bed, and asked, "Where's the ring?"

Flash, having none, quickly looked around her bedroom and offered instead a good-luck onyx stone she'd had for years. Not the kind of rock I'd hoped for, but I accepted it nevertheless, and started making lists: people to invite, people not to invite, the menu, the music. . . .

Flash wanted to celebrate our engagement in a different, more traditional manner, but I pushed her aside. "There's no time for that now," I said, reaching over her flawless back for paper and pen. "I've got a wedding to plan."

As the weeks passed, I kept waiting for Flash to surprise me with an engagement ring. When none appeared, I began dropping hints. I sang "Diamonds are a Girl's Best Friend" when we showered together. I said, "Give me a ring sometime" when she left for work. When Flash asked me if I had plans for Saturday night, I told her I had a previous engagement. All to no avail.

Finally we went to visit our local lesbian jeweler to choose our wedding rings. In the excitement of choosing matching gold bands, the matter of my engagement ring was simply forgotten. Flash wanted us to start wearing our rings right away, but I was stern. "We can't wear them until we're married."

"Can we try them on?" Flash asked. We did and they looked gorgeous. "Let's just wear them out to the car," Flash said. "Let's just wear them until I take you home." "Let's just wear them while we do it." From that day forth we never took off our rings. Not even when I brought Flash home to meet the folks. You would think that my mother would notice a gold band on the ring finger of her only daughter's left hand. But you see, my family invented the "Don't ask, don't tell" policy.

Flash was amazed. "You mean you're not going to tell your parents about the wedding?"

"Of course not," I said. "Then I'd have to invite them."

"But who's going to give you away?" she asked.

I didn't hesitate. "My therapist."

In the months to come, Flash and I met with a printer, a florist, a photographer, a caterer, a bartender, a deejay, a band, a rabbi, a hairdresser, a dressmaker, a shoemaker, and a tailor. We compiled a guest list of our 200 nearest and dearest, none of whom bothered to send back their little reply cards that were enclosed with their invitations complete with envelope and LOVE stamp. We tried to explain to our caterer, who desperately needed a head count, that lesbians think RSVP stands for "Respond Slowly vs. Promptly," but she was not amused.

Then before I knew it, Flash and I were standing under the *chuppah*, her best butch to our left, my dyke of honor to our right. We were surrounded by our loved ones who all wore their finest: everything from cut-off shorts and combat boots to high heels and velvet gowns. And those were just the boys. The girls wore T-shirts that said, "But Ma, she *is* Mr Right," or "Monogamy equals Monotony" depending on their point of view. Soon the rabbi started the ceremony and I started to cry. Then the rabbi started to cry. Then Flash, who is too butch to cry, had an allergy attack.

When things calmed down, Flash and I said our vows, and kissed. After we were pronounced Butch and Bride, the party went wild. Flash and I were hoisted up on chairs and paraded around for all to see. Our friends toasted us and danced circles around us. The food was so fabulous, even the vegetarians sampled the swan-shaped chopped liver centerpiece. Both wedding cakes (one traditional, the other sugar-, wheat-, and dairy-free) were divine. I tossed my bouquet and Flash threw my garter. We smile so much our faces hurt.

At the end of the day, we drove off to a nearby hotel. I didn't want to take off my wedding gown yet, so Flash worked around it. We fell asleep in each other's arms and we've slept that way ever since.

I sigh with contentment as I look at the clock on the night table. It is 12:27 and Flash is still deep in dreamland. There'll be plenty of time to celebrate tomorrow. Maybe I'll even surprise my beloved with breakfast in bed.

But the surprise is on me. When I open my eyes the next morning, I see a vision of loveliness: Flash, handsome in her silk bathrobe, stands before me holding a breakfast tray. "Happy anniversary," she says.

I ooh and aah over the fresh coffee, the bagel and lox, the red rose. "What's this?" I ask, holding up a small gift box.

"Remember the night I proposed to you?" Flash says. "I never forgot what you said."

"I said yes."

"No you didn't," Flash says. "You said, 'Where's the. . . .'"

"Ring! Oh my god!" I tear open the box and gasp at a beautiful diamond ring. At last, the rock I have always wanted. "Is it too late to get engaged?" Flash asks. I grab her by the neck and kiss her in reply. My butch. I think I'll keep her.

Vacation Lovers

Nisa Donnelly

Vacation lovers show each other only the best sides of themselves: the brazen, beautiful, beatific sides; the playful, adventuresome, fearless, joyful sides; the sides that run and grasp and clutch, hungry for flesh, the way large cats hunger for meat. They consume each other's flesh, become the sun. The world falls away until only they are the world. They are no more real. No more responsible, except to that moment. No more mommy or wife, teacher, banker, friend. They are only self, beautiful and stark, starving for touch. They are prisoners of time, although time twists, like models of DNA. A minute becomes a lifetime, stretches, then snaps back again: once, twice, a dozen times, until they are no longer certain even of the day. Is it Thursday, they ask, or only Wednesday? They count days like a miser. Then hours. Finally minutes. Until one or the other steps into the long white jetway, vanishing.

► ► ►

The red corset started it all. Slick as an open cunt, the color of blood. Tiny red flowers march and scatter and flow across the slick fabric that hugs her waist, clutches her breasts, pushing them up like demanding hands, offerings to passion. The woman she was supposed to love, but did no longer – in truth never had – declared it "silly," a "waste of money."

"If you bought that for me, it won't work."

No, not for you, she thought, but did not say. There was so little left to say. "For me," she wanted to say, "I bought it for me." Instead, she lied: "I just thought it was pretty." The woman she could no longer stand to have touch her, who had already left but who still cluttered the house with her lies and possessions and presence, relented.

"Where did you get it?" knowing that the Kmart and Wal-Mart and Bargain Bin, the Costco and Home Depot and Office Max – the only stores they ever frequented, indeed the only stores there were in this foresaken cow town where she found herself by accident or painful design (she no longer knew which) – did not stock red satin corsets, the color of blood, slick like an open cunt.

"The Internet. You can find anything on the Internet." And the woman she was supposed to love but could no longer, nodded, a guilty smile tugging at her eyes, remembering the lies she herself spun two, three, four times a night to the straight woman in the next town. (Bad attempts at poetry. Worse attempts at love. No one was supposed to know. Everyone knew.)

The Internet is how the world comes to cow towns. She had found the black satin ball gown with the fishtail skirt there too – had outbid a drag queen – and the fishnet stockings and leather gloves, red, too, like the corset. And finally, she had found a lover there, as well. She did not tell the woman she had never loved any of that, of course, although it wouldn't have mattered. She needed that secret, the way she needed the ball gown tucked in the far back of the closet behind the rest of her city clothes, the rest of her real life.

In the afternoon, when the sun hung warm and easy across her office, she wrote fantasies into the computer screen, turned words into caresses, flailed flesh with promises, then sent them across 2,000 miles of phone line. The words were coy and sharp and hungry and open. They came easy, the words. She had not come in a long, long time.

The woman she had never seen sent words back. It mattered. They were no more real to each other's real lives than ghosts; apparitions of pure lust burning like meteors through cyberspace. "Will you," the Internet woman would write, "play with me, fuck me, open me, plunge fingers and fists inside me, bite me, bruise me, hold me? Will you push the world away? Will you wear the red corset for me?"

It was a game. It was not a game.

The woman she had never loved, who had brought her to this place at the end of the world, took herself away, piece by piece, until finally it was settled, a few boxes and trinkets left behind, gathering dust and rats' nests in the barn. They encounter each other infrequently, and then only with the uncomfortable pause, as if the mind is asking: Is it someone I've known? Yes. Long ago. No more.

The woman whose words slid and skidded across the miles finally turned from words to flesh, to open cunt, to breasts white and hard, nipples too pink, but not as pink as they would become. They became vacation lovers. Tied by lust as surely as they are separated by distance. They plotted weekends in cities, rented rooms in beautiful hotels overlooking the sea. The view matters. They seldom leave the room. Hang the "Do Not Disturb" sign on the door – mostly in English, sometimes in Spanish – and create their own world. "This is our home," she says to the woman she found on the Internet, the one who slides her hands across the red satin of the corset, the one who plunges tiny hands into red wet cunt.

They shut out the present, when they are together, a few days, a few hours. They count the minutes. They ask: "Is today Wednesday, or is it Thursday?" They do not say "already," although the word hovers around them like fog on a beach. They laugh when the hotel maid, finally frustrated by the "Do Not Disturb" sign that never leaves the door, finally calls, finally asks, tentative: "When will you be away, so that we might service the room, madam?" When they do leave, finally, pink and slick and still aching with the want that never quite subsides, they hold hands. The gay doorman smiles with recognition. It is a good hotel, the kind that keeps doormen and maids in uniform. The kind that does not ask them to be quiet, that instead leaves the rooms on either side of them unoccupied so as not to disturb the other guests with the howls and the laughter.

They offer up lust and flesh. They count hours and minutes. They deny what they know is inevitable. They watch the sky turn, pink to gold then blue. They watch skin turn, pink to red, then darker with stains of passion. They pull each other into a fire so hard that the passage itself leaves bruises that will last for days, which they wish would last longer, mementoes.

Appetites are never really quiet for long. The hunger grows again, slow and sure as air. And they run back to the good hotel, with the good bed, past the doorman. Kiss in the elevator. Curse how slowly it rises. If its walls were not made of glass they would . . . they would . . . they are thieves. They awaken each other with kisses and sighs, touch each other in ways that only new lovers can and do. It is always that way. It is not real, the way words spelled out on a computer screen are not real. Words do not feed what the flesh needs, what it hungers for. They know that the word is not enough. L-i-p-s spelled out on a screen do not kiss, cannot touch, are not real. But for this moment, they are beyond words. For this moment, they feel real.

Vacation lovers are not real. They show only the best sides to each other, the playful, the adventuresome, the rash, the brazen, the beautiful. Vacation lovers turn to each other in the night, always open, always hungry, always willing to push time, which twists back on itself. They are as real as the world they make, as real as the best and beautiful can be. They are not tarnished by the banal, the tedious. The lies they tell each other do not matter. They long for each other, on nights when the light falls long and gentle across empty rooms, across rooms where the women they are supposed to love but cannot or do not or will not any longer sit watching television. Rooms no less empty because another is there. Their own fingers gently trace where the bruises were, bringing back the memories. They sigh. They count the days, then weeks, hours then days, minutes then hours. Until vacation. Until they can become as real lovers as they ever will be. Again.

To Bear Fruit

Terrie Hamazaki

Harue sits on a wooden stool, scrubbing her arms with hot soapy water. Her hand towel fits neatly in her palm. She keeps her head down and averts her gaze from the other girls who wash themselves with similar vigor. High-pitched chatter bounces off the tiled floor and is absorbed by the wooden walls. A row of windows cut near the nine-foot ceiling allows steam that rises from the hot water to escape. Over one hundred girls who live in the candy factory dormitories bathe together at the public *ofuro* in a nightly ritual that allows for gossip and mutual support. The row of girls at the faucets turn as if one body, and each passes her towel to the girl behind her, so that aching young backs can be scrubbed in curious massage. Grateful sighs and hoarse grunts underlie the subtle whimpering of homesick teenagers.

Harue, close to the end of the line, feels a blunt fingertip tap her shoulder. She turns to a girl, one of her roommates, who smiles at her with prominent eyeteeth that gleam in the early evening light.

"*Senaka shite-ageyo,*" the girl says, pulling Harue's towel away from her. She rinses it once, wrings it out and, without waiting for a response to her invitation, scrubs Harue's back.

"*Dokkara kiteru-no,*" the girl continues, wanting to know where Harue is from.

"*Kagoshima,*" is Harue's quiet reply. She has been teased before by these girls on coming from a place in Japan that is legendary for its strange dialect, so different from the rest of the country.

"*Jado,*" the girl teases, using the Kagoshima phrase for "that's right." She pushes Harue's shoulder forward. "*Jado,*" she repeats, laughing.

Harue's back muscles tighten. She is uncomfortable with anyone touching her, especially one who teases. "*Arigato,*" she says, reaching back and pulling the towel out of the girl's hands.

The girl, surprised at Harue's lack of manners, whispers something to another girl behind her and they both giggle.

Harue blushes. She wipes at the moisture on her face, a mixture of sweat and tears and turns toward the taps, cleansing her body with water from her cupped hands.

"*Hai-yo! Yukkuri, yukkuri!*" The factory supervisor's voice booms from outside the bathhouse, frightening some of the girls who quickly rinse their bodies of soap in preparation to leave for their shared dorm rooms.

The supervisor enters the *ofuro* with a trio of older girls who follow her, single file. They find a spot at the almost vacant line of faucets. Mai, the tallest and most beautiful of the trio, bends her head closer to the supervisor's ear before nodding in silent greeting at the younger girls who stare at them open-mouthed. The conversation of the higher-ranked is muted, not the boisterous chattering of before.

Harue feels frozen to her seat. She is not her usual self. Back in Kagoshima, the boys were afraid to taunt her for she was not averse to pulling hair or kicking a boy if he dared to pick on some girl who couldn't defend herself. Her faded dresses were often dirtier when she got home than when she left in the morning. Her hand-me-down shoes were scuffed and worn. She used to tease that one boy, *Minoru,* his ponderous name meaning "to bear fruit." A stocky boy who used to pick on the smaller children. *Minoran,* she'd say, changing the suffix to reflect the verb's negative. Doesn't bear fruit. Infertile. Impotent. She'd dared his balled up fists and bull head.

It's not the same here at the candy factory where she's moved to, having quit school to help her mother support the family. Harue feels shrunken. A long strand of hair falls out of the tight bun on her head and she lets it cover her eyes. She glances up and sees Mai's head drop down onto her chest. Harue imagines the heart-shaped face, atop its broken stem, struggling to awaken in the dawn's light. Her breath stops when Mai's head bobs up, turns, brown eyes catching her gaze.

"*Kagoshima kara kiteru-no.*" A strange girl walks across the floor toward Harue, her large breasts swaying with each step of her heavy tread. Another of her work mates wanting to laugh at her origins.

"*Hai,*" Harue begins, her soft reply audible in the sudden silence of the *ofuro.*

The supervisor has disrobed to reveal broad shoulders and a distended belly. Low murmurs fill the cavernous space, rise in their petty echo. Harue stares with the other bathers as their leader, oblivious or indifferent to the words muttered behind hands raised to glittering faces, rinses her body before entering the bath. Her well-muscled back ripples underneath her own ministrations. The fact of her bathing after her charges does not go unnoticed. Her place in the strictly coded hierarchy within the workings of the factory has fallen with this pregnancy, rumored to be caused by one of the machinists, a married man with two grown children.

Harue watches Mai rise from her stool and, joining the supervisor, takes her towel from her, rinses her back. *Irezumi.* The whispered word floats and spins in the wet humidity of the *ofuro.* The mythical invisible tattoo, said to remain hidden until its wearer immerses herself in a hot bath and emerges with a red canvas body, slowly appears on the supervisor's back, in stark white-ink relief against her flushed skin. The promise of a crane in mid-flight, with its sleek body and majestic headpiece beckons in the moonlight.

Harue can see the sharp tip of the crane's beak with each downward stroke of the towel in Mai's graceful hands.

Behind City Windows

Barrie Jean Borich

I.

Behind an uncurtained window in a midwestern American city, a woman is running a bath. The water runs hot and her lavender salts dissolve quickly. The fragrance fills the steamy room – hot scent, dusky and sweet. Her robe is ripped under her right arm and frayed above her left knee. When it was new, she left it on during lovemaking more than once, and remembers the satin collar falling off her shoulder, the purple sash still tied around her waist as her tight nipples and clenching pussy pushed up toward hands, mouth, dildo, and how later the robe smelled of it. She thinks of buying a new robe. Something fuzzy? An animal print? But she can't imagine wearing any other.

She lets the robe slip to floor. She has turned out the lights and the windows glow from streetlamps in the alley. Her arms are scratched, from pruning the rose bushes. She never was very careful. Her knuckles and elbows are muddy. Her stomach sags a bit, and her thighs are thicker than they used to be, but her breasts still stand up, and her nipples are still dark brown and wider than two quarters. The tub is full and purple in the low light. She fingers the water, checking the temperature, then strokes one nipple tight.

Once she's immersed, she strokes the other nipple with coarse fingers until it is tight too. She pictures the neighbor she spoke with that afternoon, over the yard fence. She knows the woman has a husband. She doesn't expect anything to happen. Yet here, alone in her fragrant tub, she sees that woman's shoulder muscles, her high, firm breasts with pink nipples tight as marbles, and a clear purple dildo rising between her legs as if it were always a part of her. The woman in the tub spreads her thighs and tosses her ankles over the sides. Her fingers slide inside. Her mouth opens and closes without sound as steam obscures her window.

2.

Two women sit at opposite ends of their dining room table. The curtains are open. One sits up straight and pounds her fists on the tabletop. The water glasses pitch and slide. The other has her head in her hands. Her short bleached hair stands up between her fingers like brittle grass.

A few weeks from now, these two will no longer share this table. The tabletop pounder will be living with her brother on the other side of the river. The other will sit at this same table with a real estate agent, will realize the house has tripled in value since the time she moved in with her then-new lover. She will be able to afford a small condo downtown with a view of the skyline. She will imagine inviting in someone new, to see the view, once this trouble is finally done.

But first she has to live through this miserable night, ice pelting the windows, a woman she used to love for the smooth intelligence of her face now contorted and unrecognizable. The blonde woman has her head in her hands because she can't stand to look at her lover, as withered-looking as the old lady sculptures she remembers from when she was a girl in Brown County, Indiana – dolls with aprons and straw brooms, their wrinkles formed from the petrified edges of dried apples.

The first meal they'd shared at this table was spinach pasta, tossed with olive oil and clam sauce. They'd sat side by side, toasted their new home with juice in fluted glasses. Their thighs and bare feet pressed and rubbed each other's, and they fed each other mouthfuls of noodles, kissed, licked juice off the edges of each other's lips. The one who would later become so petrified was relaxed that night, her long clean hair pulled back in an uneven ponytail. They stripped off each other's clothes, their bodies slippery and flexible in each other's hands. They came together hard and loud right there, on the other side of the polished wood archway, on the cool dusty floor of their new living room, between the unpacked boxes that started out that morning in two separate apartments. They didn't clean up dinner until morning.

They won't do the dishes this night either, except for one glass that rattles right off the edge and falls broken to the wooden dining room floor, as the pounder, her hair flying loose and dirty, shouts so loudly people walking their dogs outside can hear. That water glass seems to rise of its own accord, hovering for a moment, a satellite of unhappiness before breaking apart.

3.

Our sunset-colored walls look as bright as a cut orange from the street outside our house. Behind the old lace curtains I dream of replacing, I am watching a dirty movie with my lover. The woman on the screen has long blonde hair that she winds around her neck and lets fall over one shoulder, to keep it out of the way. Her professional name is Kinky. Her play partner's name is Buster. Kinky is naked and balances on her hands and knees, her ass spread before the camera like the meeting of two moons. Buster is a small-breasted butch wearing nothing but a necktie, a leather harness, and peach-colored dildo as long as a small woman's forearm.

My hair is short, but I imagine it falls long over my right shoulder. My ample-bodied lover of fifteen years wears boxers and a T-shirt, but I imagine she has on nothing but a tie. My lover's dildo feels as long as a forearm. Kinky and I move in tandem, our asses held by strong hands, our nipples tight as gravel, her cry high and breathless, mine as long and low as a locomotive whistle.

Outside, a car's headlights blink and vanish. Curtains close. Lights behind windows turn on or off as the city moans and settles.

The Bus

Maria de los Rios

The top of my head boils under the late afternoon sun. The rusted transmission cranks. The old engine struggles. Its heavy metal body, stuffed with people, chickens, pigs, coughs uphill. Struggling to catch up, my right hand reaches out, ready to grab the rusted rod and propel my body inside. I know Eloina is not going to stop for anyone. That's the way it is in this barrio: you never stop. You keep on racing, keep on moving. If you stop, you risk missing the bus, life altogether. As the wind, humid and hot, blows the surface of the earth, declaring the beginning of the wet season, I take a deep breath, jump, snatch the hand bar, and stumble my body up the three tall steps.

"*Buenos tardes, Mariel.*"

"*Buenisimas, Eloina,*" I respond, giggly. Gabriel Garcia Marquez's *one hundred years of solitude* meet Alejo Carpentier's *lost steps* in my depths as the yellow butterflies of anticipation flap their minute wings inside my chest, making the cocoon of fear transform into the larva of uncertainty.

"*Y a uste' que bicho le pico que anda tan nerviosa?*" (What insect stung you that you seem so nervous?) Eloina's squinting eyes give me a look.

I want to tell Eloina all about Alina. I bite my tongue instead. What does Eloina care? I know she is going to tell me what everybody in *el Socorro* says: "Step down from that cloud *mija*, get yourself a good man, and secure your future."

A fat hand with a thick lifeline, rich Venus mound, and three chubby fingers waits for the bus fare. I search my pockets, place my last five *medios* into Eloina's palm. *Como quien no come cuento,* she counts the *medios*, deposits them in her coin belt, and shifts into second gear.

Sweat droplets wander down her wide forehead to her protruding cheeks. Some travel past her neck. Others linger on her thick upper lip, hopelessly waiting for something. Still others surrender, dripping down her chest, meandering the road of her cleavage until they get lost behind her flowery blouse. She shifts into third gear. Eloina's round and full *toronjas* bounce up and down, right to left, left to right, in circles.

I grab the metal bar, lean against the zesty armpit of a construction worker. She flirts. I smile. Aroused by women's sights and body odors, I try to stand aloof. As I fight my sexual urges, a soothing voice surfs across the high tide of flesh, sexual flare, menstrual blood, chicken sweat, and pig breath: "Mariel."

Armed with a fearless look, my body pushes against the current through an ocean of naked, hairy armpits. The undertow pulls me back as the vehicle slows down, approaching another stop. Conquering the wave of flesh that ebbs and flows as the bus moves uphill, I stubbornly push forward: past the young male with the *'chupamelo papi'* tattooed next to a bleeding heart on his lower arm, holding the fighting rooster with the black hood and the tied legs who's all excited by the horny chickens that screech inside their cage, held prisoners by an old woman with more teeth than a dog fight, finally reaching a harbor of joy as my eyes lower to encounter Alina's.

In spite of the asphyxiating humidity, her black pearls glow with insatiable hunger behind the bush of shiny, wet brown curls. With a swift move, she pushes away the old man sitting to her right. Convinced that there is no room for disagreement, cursing, he joins the standing crowd.

Smiling at the young girl with the dirty nose wearing bright pink Foster Grants, I force myself under his arm, reaching the seat. My ass rests on the cracked vinyl surface with exposed reddish-brown coils. Crimson-colored lips gently part, drawing desire with a capital D. Wanting to smear her lipstick, I stare, hypnotized by the slightly open, plump, and inviting rim.

As I lean to kiss Alina's cheek, my mouth salivates at the sight of round, full breasts bouncing freely under the thin raw cotton shirt with the v-neck. Noticing her nipples are so hard they could pierce through the fabric, I burn with the urgency of the seventeen-year-old I was back then, craving to fuck her, not even knowing where to begin.

Providing a suitable camouflage, Alina covers our legs with her raincoat. Guiding my hand under her mini-skirt, she whispers in my ear, "I can't wait, *nena*."

Knowing that patience is not my virtue, I lean towards the dirty window, pass my right arm around her shoulders, scan the crowd, and press my body against hers. In an act of disappearance, my left hand reaches her wetland. My fingers explore her moist ravine, dive deep into her hot spring. As the bus climbs the road, leaving a tail of orange dirt, conveniently bouncing its contents about and around, her folds suck my fingers in with a steady rhythm. Like riding a rodeo horse, her juicy cunt rides my wrist. Her hands hold tight to the metal handle over the seat; her moans are lost among the convenient sound buffer provided by acute noises: metal against metal, chickens, pigs, the radio sportscaster narrating the baseball game, *"Rivera steals second base."*

Right there, in the midst of the crowd, she drenches my hand, electrifying my soul with more power than the Caroni River. She releases me, then grins. The strong and delightful scent of ripe passion fruit elates my senses. "Ashe," she wets her crimson lips. *"Como tu sabes, mami."*

Dreams of Jennifer Connelly

Gabrielle Glancy

Out over the heads of the gifted and talented, the East River snaked and glistened and the Twin Towers loomed lovingly over lower Manhattan like two brothers dressed in identical suits of silver turned gold in the light of the waning sun that broke over Coney Island, my childhood home. My classroom had the best view in the school. Often, I found my inspiration in those waters. It was against this backdrop that Jennifer Connelly came to see me one day after class. They were shooting on location, she said, and would need to spend most of the semester in Rome. Could I send her the assignments? Would I be willing to meet with her, for the week before she headed off, every day after school?

So yes, I did give Jennifer Connelly her assignments ahead of time, grudgingly. Much as I liked her and could see her sincere desire to connect with me, I resented the fact that she thought she could take my course by correspondence, though I noted that she was poised, even brilliant, and indeed, there was something unusual about her, even if she seemed a little aloof.

Until my ex-girlfriend, Martha, told me to go see *A Beautiful Mind*, I had forgotten about Jennifer Connelly completely. And now I can't forget about her at all.

Jennifer Connelly looked thin at the Academy Awards, you have to admit, and pale. Her dress was also pale, a flesh-colored chiffon with a scarf that wrapped around her neck. She's anorexic, I thought, and unhappy. This was the seed of what has become an obsession. I want to find Jennifer Connelly and offer her my help.

So I rented *Requiem for a Dream*. In this movie, Jennifer Connelly is the junkie's junkie girlfriend. She's young, untainted, and full-breasted; smart, direct, seductive. And the whole thing, as it turns out, was shot in Coney

Island, where I grew up. If you ever rent that movie, you'll see that there is a full frontal shot of Jennifer Connelly naked. She is standing in front of a full-length mirror admiring her beautiful physique. I also admire her beautiful physique.

Jennifer Connelly took my Romanticism class long-distance from Rome. I sent her the assignments and she sent me back perfectly written, perfectly typed essays on Wordsworth, Shelley, Coleridge, and Keats. I never even considered that these may have been written by her secretary or someone who was tutoring her on the set.

Recently, at a party I had at my house, a woman I dated briefly – we'll call her Good-But-Not-Very-Interesting-Poet R – overheard me talking about Jennifer Connelly. When I suggested that indeed Jennifer might be excited to hear from me, that she might gasp in breathless anticipation at my offer to meet her in L.A., I could see the sneer on Good-But-Not-Very-Interesting-Poet R's face out of the corner of my eye. Let her sneer, I thought. Personally, I don't think it's completely impossible that Jennifer Connelly will be my next girlfriend. Stranger things have happened.

Lemon Fetish

Sarah B. Wiseman

I'm a garnisher. I cut strawberries into hearts, watermelons into roses, and lemons into half-moons. Name a fruit, I've shaped it. I work in the restaurant at the golf club just down the street from the gay bar, where closeted old boys get their rocks off by looking at their buddies' asses when they bend over to make a shot. Where, if I'm lucky, the boys bring in their wives and give me a chance to have a little fun. Make the women's strawberries into breasts, their sliced lemons into cunts, with seeds for clits. Then flirt with them at the deli table.

If I'm really lucky, a bunch of dykes will come in for a meal before going out to the bar for the night. Which is how I met my last ex, Sharon. She was a short, muscled jock who captured my heart by turning the half-moon lemons I'd put on her plate into a triple citrus twist. She sent it back to the kitchen for me with a love note stuck in the toothpick from her club sandwich.

I've discovered in my time as a garnisher that most people prefer flowery strawberry and watermelon garnishes to anything citrus. But personally, I like the lemons best. Nothing sweet and syrupy. Nothing froufrou. I want something that always makes my mouth water. Pure and simple. And well, a triple citrus twist? I was hooked.

Sharon was crude. Loved hockey, playing cards, gin, and leather. Usually in that order. While we were together, my friend Janet, her long-time partner Jen, and Sharon and I started playing euchre every Thursday night. Sharon and I would share lemon gin across the table as a kind of foreplay. We'd go home to great sex, the smell of lemon on our breath. I always thought it was the lemon that intrigued Sharon. But as it turned out, she left me for a bartender three months after we met. Said alcohol was way more enticing than fruit.

When I sobbed about it to Janet, all she said was, "But what about cards night?" She had gotten attached to the game, I guess. Myself, to the lemon gin. I didn't really care about not playing euchre for a while. But Janet wouldn't let it go. She said she'd find another fourth before Thursday came around. And she held to her word. Next cards night, she and Jen dragged me to the new player's house.

"Emily will be a perfect replacement," Janet had told me on the subway ride over.

I couldn't tell if she meant as a euchre partner or as a girlfriend. Either way, Emily didn't quite fit the bill. She was tall, femme, artsy, and a bad card player. A soft-spoken, women's collective, moon circles kind of chick. Everytime we lost a hand at euchre she would touch my arm and say earnestly, "It's okay, we did our best." She screamed flowery strawberry garnishes. Not really my type.

As we played, I made eyes at Janet, trying to figure out why she thought Emily would be a perfect replacement. Don't get me wrong, I liked her well enough to begin with, she just didn't move me, sexually or otherwise.

Until, that is, the second round of cards was over.

I got up to take a leak. In her bathroom I noticed, first, the claw foot tub and hand-held showerhead. Then, a painting of a lemon hanging above the toilet. That lemon made me blush. It made me wet. It made me wish I had taken a "How to be a Drag King" course and learned how to pee standing up so I didn't have to take my eyes off that damn fine lemon while I relieved myself. And that's when it hit me about Emily. She liked it sour! Sometimes a garnish is worth a thousand words.

When I composed myself, left the bathroom and sat back down for the last game of cards, I took more notice of certain aspects of Emily's personality. Assertive; not afraid of taking risks in the game, even if she did lose them. Passionate; continually gave it her all. Creative; used to working with her hands.

At one point, Janet asked her what she'd been painting lately and I couldn't help but picture her naked breasts dangling like lemons above her paintbrush. When she said, "I love doing still life, it takes patience," all I heard was, "I love doing you, you taste perfect."

By the end of the night I was completely absorbed. I knew I couldn't leave without doing something about it. She got up to see us to the door and I headed to the bathroom one last time. The lemon stared at me, its body perfectly plump, each end pushing out into hard nipples.

I mustered up my most sultry, garnisher's voice and said, "Hey, Em, would you like to go for a drink sometime?" I practiced this line over and over again.

I also tried, "Do you play golf? I get benefits."

And, "Ya wanna get naked together in your bathroom?"

Janet and Jen were gone by the time I walked into the hallway. Emily was still standing by the door. I took a deep breath and slowly made my way towards her. She didn't know what she was in for. I crossed my fingers. Paused in front of her. She smiled.

"Uh, nice lemon," I said.

I'm not sure what I was hoping for. Maybe that she'd push me against the door, grab my crotch, and talk to me about citrus or something. But no. She just shook my hand and said thanks, good game tonight, see you next week. And then sent me on my way.

Next week? I thought. *We'll get naked together in her bathroom next week?*

I took a long walk home. When I got there, I sliced myself a piece of lemon, sucked out its bitterness, and with sticky fingers made myself come, right there in the kitchen, with the grapefruit watching.

Too Cool for School

Nairne Holtz

I hear the other girls giggle before I realize that Sister Frances is talking to me. I slide the book I'm not supposed to be reading under the front of my blazer. On pain of crucifixion, I'm not going to give it up.

"Elena, what could you be reading that is more compelling than the social and economic problems leading to the overthrow of the Russian Tsar in 1917?" Sister Frances sucks her lips in.

I look at the gouges on my desk. Behind me, I hear retching. I turn in my seat to see Mary Beth holding her hand over her mouth. As usual, she looks like a disaster. Her white school shirt isn't ironed and her long ponytail is looping out of what appears to be a rubber band. She stands up, lurches towards Sister Frances, and lifts her right hand to point to the hall.

Sister Frances sighs. "Yes, you can go to the bathroom. Let's hope this doesn't mean your school days are numbered."

I stare at Sister Frances. Two girls left school this year because they were pregnant, but the nuns never talk about it. Mary Beth could be knocked up. She *did* transfer to Our Lady of Peace after getting kicked out of public school for blowing two guys in the boy's bathroom. At least that's what everyone says. I can't figure her out. She cracks homophobic jokes about lezzie nuns, yet I catch her watching me. I don't exactly wear rainbow jewelery, but everyone knows I had a girlfriend who graduated last year.

"Elena," Sister Frances begins, but she's interrupted by the bell.

Too classic. I shake my head, take the book from my blazer and place it in my backpack. Then I join the girls bum-rushing the door.

I walk to the stone wall at the edge of school property in order to grab a butt. I don't really like smoking. I just do it to have some girls to talk to, but today no one's here. Maybe the girls are meeting some guys at the mall again. You'd think lesbianism would be rampant at a Catholic girls' school, but in fact, homosexuality is so repressed that all anyone talks about is getting with a boy.

I'm sitting on the wall, smoking a cigarette by myself, when Mary Beth jogs up to me.

"Hey Buffy, light me one, will you?" Mary Beth slouches down, placing her elbows on the stone wall.

Mary Beth calls me Buffy the Vampire because I wear black eye makeup and dye my long brown hair black. A smoke ring curls from my mouth. "Why should I?"

"Because you owe me. I saved you. I knew the bell would go so I made like one of the Bulimia Girls." Mary Beth sounds suave, but her eyes are jumping around like a puppy who wants to please me.

"Now that I know you're not going to hurt an unborn child, why not?" I set my cigarette down on the wall, take my cigarettes from my blazer pocket, then open the pack and realize it's empty. I duck my head a little. "Sorry."

"Shit," says Mary Beth. "How about you let me borrow the book that's too cool for school?"

"I can't because it's not mine."

"Well, let me see it."

I get the book from my bag and hand it to her. She pushes herself up onto the wall with her hands and begins flipping through the pages. I look at a star of puckered skin on her knee.

"Check it out, there's some girl-on-girl action. Ahem." Mary Beth holds the book out with one hand. "My schoolmate Alice was a dark handsome girl of eighteen. When we studied, she would recline her head in a languid manner on my lap and gaze at me with great fondness. One evening, she asked me to join her in bed whereupon she pressed her mouth to mine, clasped me to her bosom, and gently caressed me. These strange liberties brought warmth to my cheeks, but I found myself quite unable to make an objection as marvellous sensations grew in my cunny. Alice told me she longed for me to be a man so that I might pleasure her. 'Rub your finger on my crack – it is a jolly game, you shall see.' I thrust my fingers into her slit until she wriggled, sighed, and yielded nectar upon my hands."

Pinwheels spark between my legs. I want to kiss Mary Beth. She's not even pretty, but what she's reading has cranked me and it's right off the Richter of anything I've ever felt before.

"Then she pulled from the pillow what appeared to be a sausage, only it was made of finest vulcanized india rubber," Mary Beth stops and laughs.

"Is that something you would know about?"

I blush, but I'm furious. I hate hypocrisy. "Hardly. But I think you would."

"What the hell's that supposed to mean?"

"You did get kicked out of school for blowing two guys in the boy's washroom. So don't trip on me."

"That's bullshit. I was failing my classes. I just went into the guy's washroom for a joke and it was like, you know, the last straw. I wouldn't blow one guy, let alone two. Gross."

I do something crazy then. I grab her by the lapels of her blazer, and I kiss her. Edge my tongue under her lips. Rock hard candy sweet. Feel her large breasts locomote to my small ones. The nuns say it's a sin, but how can sin be so soft? "Is this gross?"

Mary Beth bit her lip. "No. But it's definitely too cool for school." She looks over at the yard and slides off the wall. "C'mon, let's go. Have you ever hooked off school before? You won't get in trouble if you're a first time offender."

I watch her, feeling like I'm in a funhouse. This morning she looked like any girl, but now she shimmers before me in an unexpected way. I've never skipped school, but I have to follow her. She could change her mind although something tells me she won't. I hold out my hand, and she helps me off the wall.

The Second Street Rag

Florence Grandview

She hauled out her high school annual and showed me pictures of all her friends.

Her friends Robyn, Dee Dee, and Samantha all resembled one another with brown hair combed halfway down their scowling faces.

"Hey Lenore," I said, "your friends kinda look like you."

"We're the unpopular crowd," Lenore said emphatically. "We're going places and only we know where."

I had just met Lenore at Inlet Park. I'd been brooding on my favorite bench – the one above the highway – when I had that feeling I was being watched. Then Lenore came over and introduced herself. She was wearing white jeans and a cardigan that said Royal Senior Secondary.

I wasn't surprised she was trailing her annual around because all the local schools – mine, too – had just issued them the week before. End-of-term was near, although the weather was slow to warm up.

I didn't buy an annual because I hated my school picture. I looked like I was ducking my head against a flying tomato, while trying to face the camera and smile at the same time.

"What school do you go to, anyway?" asked Lenore.

"Second Street School, across the inlet. You can almost see it from here."

"I know where it is already," said Lenore, "It's a creepy school. You're one of the unpopular girls, too, I can tell just by looking. Am I right or am I wrong?"

I was about to open my mouth but Lenore quickly added, "I think we nobodies from all the schools could get together and outnumber the snobs. It wouldn't be hard."

"I'm not unpopular," I said, "I'm in the drama club and I write for the school paper – *The Second Street Rag.* I write poetry, too. Next term I'm going to start a poetry club."

Part of that was a fib. I was in the drama club all right, but I was in the grunt section that stayed behind the scenes and built sets and moved them around. We never got to be out there on stage, and no one else even knew we were in the club.

I also wrote for *The Second Street Rag*, but the only kids who did that were the bookworms with horn-rimmed glasses, like me. As for poetry, I knew darn well I wouldn't be able to start a club, although I often said I would. None of the girls I was acquainted with wrote poetry; they only talked about boys.

I knew of two boys at our school who were poets – they both had long hair and leather headbands with studs – but they wouldn't even talk to me. I was too unpopular. Lenore could tell just by looking, so I didn't know whether I liked her yet. I'd never be able to let my guard down if she were too perceptive.

"I'm going to start a club, too," said Lenore. "The Anti-Pollution Club. My friends are already queued up to join. But none of the snobby kids are allowed. They're not interested in important things like ecology, anyway. They're too occupied looking at themselves in the mirror."

"If you're such a nobody, how come you're wearing your high school sweater, Lenore? Isn't that a bit cliquey?" I sounded meaner than I'd intended.

"Not at my school. Anyway, it was given to me. By Robyn." She flipped through her annual again to the page where Robyn's gloomy visage was displayed.

"At my school, only the cheerleader-types wear school cardigans," I explained, "like this one girl called Gloria. She and her pals all wear the same thing, and no one dares copy them."

"Well, how about forget them and come to our first meeting of the Anti-Pollution Club?" said Lenore, with more enthusiasm than I was accustomed to. "We're meeting at my house tonight. If you want to join us, I'll give you my address."

▸ ▸ ▸

I told Lenore I didn't want to go, and she didn't give me her address.

▸ ▸ ▸

The following Monday at noon hour, I was sitting at my usual place in the school cafeteria – the Nobody Table. I turned and saw Gloria the Cheerleader waving at me. "Come and sit with us."

"Me?" I asked, as I made my way through the chatter and the clanging utensils.

"Yes, you. Last Friday, Mr Holmes told the class how impressed he was with your journalism. He was surprised we didn't even know you. I mean, we know you, but you know what I mean, we don't hang around with you."

Mr Holmes was one of the English Lit teachers at Second Street School, and most of the girls had a crush on him because he resembled Lord Byron's portrait in *Collier's Encyclopedia*.

"We tried to find you on the weekend," said Gloria, "but we didn't know where to look."

"Well, I usually go to Inlet Park," I explained. "I sit on the bench that has Highway 49 on one side and Crystal Inlet on the other. That's my favorite place to find inspiration."

I thought I saw one of Gloria's friends roll her eyes, but maybe not. Whenever I was nervous, I imagined things.

"You were sitting there by yourself?" Gloria leaned forward.

"Actually, no, I wasn't. I met a girl from Royal called Lenore. When I first met her, I didn't like her, but I've found myself thinking about her ever since. She's different –"

"Whoa, wait a minute here," Gloria raised her voice, "Lenore from Royal High? Kind of stocky, with frizzy hair and a bad complexion?"

"Yes, that sounds like her. She's starting an Anti-Pollution Club. Hey, you know her?"

"Anti-Pollution Club." She turned to address her friends now. "How about the Lezzie Club?"

Her friends began to snort and giggle, and Gloria turned back to me. "Lenore and her friends are all lezzies. Everyone knows that, you Clue." Her chair grated against the floor as she pushed it back.

Incredibly, the bell rang right about then, so I didn't have to respond. I could get up and head towards home room, which is exactly what I did. "I'd rather have one Lenore than ten Gloria's," is the thought that carried me down the hall.

Unfortunately, I'd kind of blown it with Lenore, refusing to join her club and not having her address. I consoled myself by watching the jeweled glow of the sun against the classroom windows.

Under a Blue Sky

Melinda Johnston

"Have you ever kissed a boy?" Christine asked.

"No," Jules replied.

"Me neither." Christine stretched her slim arms toward the sky.

The sky was a rich, flat blue, like a nursery wall painted for a doting rich parent by a skilled worker. The blue stretched in a perfect bowl with only a small puff of white cloud to mar it, like a careless assistant dinging the wall with a ladder on his way out. The same blue was reflected in Jules's eyes, staring up like a fallen paint chip from the fragrant, spiky golden brown nest she'd carved from Mr O'Reilly's back hay field.

Jules was lying back, looking up at the sky. On her stomach, resting against Jules's slight pouch of baby fat, was the tawny-gold head of Christine Bouychuck, her hair fanned out just the way an art director from a Pert commercial would have placed it. At thirteen, Christine was pretty much what Nabokov must have imagined when he wrote Lolita. Jules and Christine were best friends. They had been so ever since they'd met two years ago, both celebrating their eleventh birthdays with a pizza and pool party at the local rec centre. Beautiful Christine was the leader, and gangly Jules, who became uncharacteristically mute whenever Chris tossed her long hair, was her devoted sidekick. Right from the first day.

Now, as they lay basking in the sun, waiting for the pot brownies Jules had stolen from her brother to kick in, Jules felt a peculiar, stirring, soaring feeling in her body that couldn't be from the marijuana. It had started when she smelled the sweet scent of Christine's fruit shampoo mixed with sun-warmed hay, just before she'd extracted the squished lump of soggy brownie from her pocket, with the expression of a puppy who's just realized that chewing on his master's Prada wallet wasn't a good idea. Undeterred, Christine had divided the mess and presented it on the sticky baggy with the air of a hostess serving high tea on fine china.

"Well," Christine persisted, "wouldn't you like to?"

"Um," Jules was sure the brownie was kicking in now – that was why she was tingling, right? – "Most of the boys at school are pretty gross." She reached her hand out, and began to stroke Chris's hair. She felt her mouth go dry, and lost herself in the feel of Christine's fine hair slipping slowly through her fingers.

Chris giggled, her head bobbing against Jules's tummy. The sensation started Jules laughing too, giggling helplessly, until she began to cough and gasp.

"Picture Shamus's pimply face coming for you. . . ." Christine stuck out her tongue and made a face, causing Jules to clutch her stomach and shake soundlessly, too out of breath to laugh.

"With his braces, with all the green stuff stuck in them." Jules was practically sobbing. At last the laughter died away, and a silence fell between them. Jules snuggled back into the hay, listening to the breeze play among the grass. All at once, she became aware of her body. It felt heavy and tingly, and strange pulses were beating in places she hadn't quite figured out the purpose of. "Still," she ventured, "I wonder what it would be like?"

Christine flipped over. "Wanna try?" Her eyes glittered, and her red mouth looked full and fresh. New. Jules, unable to speak past the lump in her throat, nodded.

Christine pounced with the slightly uncoordinated grace of a floppy kitten batting a scrap of paper. She sprang on top of Jules, her long hair falling down on either side of Jules's head, sealing them in a fruit-scented, tawny-gold chamber. Christine smiled and slowly lowered her red, cupid's bow lips onto Jules's mouth. She was soft and gentle, and Jules felt suspended, as though she were floating in a warm bath inches above the ground. When Christine gently inserted an exploring tongue between Jules's lips, electrical pulses streamed down Jules's arms and legs, and she felt as though her brain was sailing straight up like a helium balloon released by an overexcited child.

Christine raised her head from Jules's mouth and stared for a moment at the expression in Jules's chipped-sky eyes, then lifted herself up, off. As the warm caramel curtains lifted away, Jules felt as though the sunshine that bathed her face was emanating from her heart, not from the sky. Christine stood and spun away, arms out, twirling and twirling herself around in exuberant joy. Jules lay still, her mouth zinging with the imprint of Christine's kiss, her heart spinning and soaring in time with the pirouettes of the golden girl above her.

Magnesia

McKinley M. Hellenes

Caroline Murphy. The most beautiful girl I know. She spends every lunch hour turning pirouettes on the lawn in front of school. Her hair is blonde, and her breasts small and firm – they never so much as budge when she lifts her arms above her head to turn cartwheels on the grass. I like to sit with my back against the library wall, watching Caroline, imagining her breasts in my hands, performing very different acrobatics above me in my bed.

The cement is cool against my back. My arms are bare, and the sun is kissing me. Caroline is sweating a little. The curve of her armpit, with its little patch of downy blonde fuzz, is alluring. Caroline stretches her body backwards into a perfect arc, her fingertips meeting the ground beneath her shoulder blades. She holds the pose for a few seconds before collapsing gracefully onto her side. She laughs at herself, rolls over, and snakes her way across the short distance to me on her elbows and knees. I wonder whether her boyfriend has ever seen her do that. The way her long braid falls against her collarbone makes me want to fuck her brains out. I hate her boyfriend, passionately, and without reservation.

"How's Brody?" I say to her, taking care to ungrit my teeth, pretending I am yawning as I say it.

She makes a face, but her shining eyes betray her, betray us both. "Okay, I guess. He hates that I never stay over, but my parents would kill me. Literally, they would *kill* me."

"So you're fucking him, then?" I narrow my eyes, pretending to block out the sun with my arm.

She makes another face. "You *know* I hate that word."

"Yeah," I say, shrugging. She always says things in italics. If language had a font, her words would be punctuated with little hearts, or small, perfectly shaped bubbles. She would say everything in daffodil yellow, or aquamarine. I shove my hand into the pocket of my shorts, where my cigarettes are making a fairly conspicuous bulge. I take a cig out of the pack and clamp it, James Dean style, in the corner of my mouth. "So, are you?" I say, lighting it.

She makes her third face, but smiles and blushes guiltily. I want to tell her that her dress is unchaste. I know she thinks it is. She thinks it doesn't matter whether everyone can see her panty lines through the sheer fabric – at least she is wearing underwear, and anyway, her dresses have little pink flowers on them, and therefore radiate nothing but virtue. I know how she thinks. That white cotton isn't naughty, that knee-highs are sensible. The girl wears Mary Janes, for Christ's sake. I exhale smoke slowly through my nostrils and cock my eyebrow suggestively, but Caroline Murphy is unmoved by my passion-play. She picks a minute particle of grass off her filmy white breast with precise fingernails. I try again.

"Does he go down on you?"

"Ewww, of *course* not!"

"But you go down on him, am I right?"

She shrugs. "I don't know. I guess so. But I don't *like* it, or anything." She screws up her face, and her nose wrinkles up like a small pink toe in bathwater. "I mean, why would I, right?" She looks to me for confirmation, as though I know exactly what she's talking about. Which I do, of course – but only theoretically.

I shrug non-committally, but what I am really thinking of is some guy's gristly red penis in Caroline's mouth, her big eyes watering, her gag reflex asserting itself in perfect time to the thrust of his hips. I want to puke. And I also want to put my hand up her dress. So I do. I reach over, and caress the hem of her dress softly with the tip of my finger. She watches my hand, even flinches ever so slightly, but she doesn't protest, so I place my palm flat against her knee, and slide my fingers up her thigh. I do it slowly, so she will know exactly where it's going. Her skin is soft, warm, like the smooth flat rocks I used to lay on at the beach when I was a kid. My hand makes a detour, and my fingers graze her panty line. I stroke the place where her thigh meets her hip, my eyes never leaving her face.

"What are you *doing?*" She whispers suddenly, frantically pushing her dress down, as though she has just noticed its ascent.

I don't say anything. Both my hands are grabbing her behind the knees, and Caroline Murphy is on her back in the grass. We are behind the building, no one will see us, though I don't particularly care. She makes another feeble attempt to push me away, but I have her panties down around her ankles so fast all she can do is lay there like a turtle turned on its shell. Her thighs are soft against the sides of my face. I can feel the surge of her muscles ebbing and flowing against my ears like a tide that can't decide whether it's coming or going. Her dress blows above my head like a pinwheel in a rainstorm. Salt water flows down my chin and then recedes.

▸ ▸ ▸

The next week, Caroline isn't in school, and never will be again. At least, that's what everyone is saying. I spend my lunch hour hunched against the library wall, smoking and fantasizing about her in her new school uniform. On the way home, I see her in every school bus window, head downcast, resting itself against the glass. Every blonde teenager in a plaid skirt quickens my pulse. And when I light my cigarette, I no longer clamp it between my teeth like James Dean. I clamp it between my teeth like my face between the thighs of Caroline Murphy.

It will become a life-long affliction.

True Romance

Connie Chapman

Susie slid her bike to a stop in front on her house. Leaping off, she knocked down the kick stand and ran up the steps, clutching a brown paper bag to her budding chest. I followed, grabbing hold of her blue sweatshirt as we ran up the stairs to her second floor bedroom.

Susie and I had been best friends for three months, ever since we started junior high and seventh grade. We'd been conspiring for the past two weeks to get hold of a *True Romance*. Today, we pooled our allowances then went to Keely's Drugs and bought one, making sure we didn't know the clerk.

Giggling, she grasped my hand in hers as she jumped on her double bed and tore open the paper bag, pulling me next to her. For the next hour, we lay on her bed, taking turns reading *True Romance* to each other. My face was flushed and I found myself wriggling every time Susie read me a passage. I looked over. Her light brown hair fell forward and covered one eye. Her other one was large and bright, matching the two crimson circles on her cheeks.

"Oh, I'd love to be kissed like that." Susie pushed the hair back behind her ear.

"I heard Gentry and Ellen talking at recess today and you know what they do? They practice with each other," I said, holding my breath.

"Oh," she said, drawing in air so quickly she sounded like she was sipping through a straw. Susie dropped the magazine on the bed and jumped on top of me, pushing my shoulders back against her pillow. I could smell Jean Naté on her pillow and wafting down from her neck. Her shoulder-length hair touched my cheeks, leaving tingles all over my face. Susie pressed her tightly closed lips hard against mine. I squirmed under the pressure. I could feel her small breasts push into mine and I definitely liked the way her body molded into me. The kiss wasn't great, though.

I pushed her face away. "My turn." I flipped Susie over onto her back and climbed on top of her, one leg between hers, the other next to her body.

"No spit," she giggled as I reached behind me with one hand and loosened the rubber band holding my hair in a blonde ponytail. I leaned over and brushed my hair across her face.

"Oh, goosebumps." Susie wriggled under me as she laughed and shook her head from side to side. Her movements tickled me back, so I did it again. I gently turned her head towards me, leaned over and gave her lips a gentle brush. She lay still. Then I kissed her cheek and each closed eyelid. I felt her shoulders relax, so I kissed her lips again, this time letting mine linger on hers. As I moved my mouth off, I felt her respond. This time I decided to kiss like the magazine described — long and deep. I wasn't sure what deep meant, so I just let myself do what felt wonderful. Her lips parted ever so slightly. Her taste, a combination of Juicy Fruit and lemon sour balls, thrilled me. I placed my hand under her head, cradling it as I savored her taste and explored her mouth with my tongue.

"That's good," Susie whispered as I came up for a breath. "You remembered the up and down part, too."

I'd been so intent on the kiss, I wasn't aware that I'd been moving my hips up and down against hers.

"You get a funny feeling when I do that?" I asked, leaning over and kissing her neck.

"Yeah, sort of like I have to go to the bathroom, but lots better."

I kissed her again This time our lips opened even more. I loved this practice. My face felt hot and I could see Susie's cheeks were beet red.

"I want you. I want you," I said, in imitation of the story we'd read earlier.

"Oh, my love. I'm swept away." We giggled and then kissed some more. Susie's hips were now moving with mine.

"*Linda-a-a.* Your mom called and it's time for you to go home for dinner," Susie's mom yelled up the stairs.

Susie and I collapsed on the bed, laughing and panting. "You'd better go before Mom comes up here and sees the magazine."

I gathered up my jacket and books, wishing my mom had forgotten about me. I looked Susie in the eye. "That was fun. Tomorrow, let's read the next story."

Susie and I bounded down the stairs and out the front door. As I got on my red Schwinn, she leaned over and whispered in my ear, "And it will be my turn to be on top."

Susie

Corrina Hodgson

Sex was always confusing.

My older brother, Frank, starts dating Susie Martin when I'm in grade seven. Susie is the older sister of my best friend, Rosa. At first, it's strange to see her in the hallways, knowing what she looks like out of uniform and with makeup on. But I eventually get used to it and become grateful to Frank. It's like he's let me in on some secret. I know Susie is more than just another student at St Mary's – she's a girl. A real girl. Like in magazines or on TV.

One afternoon Rosa motions for me to follow her into the auditorium. We sneak through the empty seats, the baby grand covered and silent on the stage, and out a door I've never seen before. It leads to a stairwell. There are twelve steps, then a landing, then twelve steps, then a landing, all the way up – to heaven, as far as I can tell. Rosa climbs to the first landing and sits down. I sit beside her. She pulls on my shoulders and positions me in her lap.

"What are we doing?" I ask her.

"I wanna show you something," she says. She straightens my right arm and turns it so that my palm is facing the ceiling. From where I'm lying, I can see the next flight of stairs leading up, up, up. "Close your eyes," she tells me, and when I do she starts stroking the inside of my arm, near the crease of my elbow.

I snap my eyes open.

"Doesn't it feel good?" she asks.

"Yeah, I guess."

"Can't you feel it everywhere in your body?"

I close my eyes again and focus on the sensations that are jumping inside me. Her fingers continue their slow stroking, barely touching my skin.

Doing homework a couple of months earlier, I suddenly hadn't been able to sit still. It wasn't like I was hyper. Or like I was nervous about anything. It was more like I had to pee although I knew I didn't. I tried to ignore the feeling and concentrate on the math problem. *Catherine can walk at three miles an hour for two hours, then she gets tired and slows to two point five miles an hour.* I continued to shift in my seat until the seam of my pants hit a place in my crotch that made me exhale all the air out of my body. *Her friend Mary walks at one point five miles an hour for four hours at a time, after which she starts to run at a rate of two miles every nine minutes.* I gripped the edge of the desk and pushed down against the seam. I started gently rocking from side to side, feeling something important happening inside my body. *Mary and Catherine live ten miles from their school. If Mary leaves her house at ten after eight and Catherine leaves her house at ten to nine, which girl arrives at school first?* There was something gathering inside of me. Something pulling me up the harder I pushed down. I felt my body break in two. It was as though I was climbing into my own chest, my belly button inching its way toward my throat, my neck trying to shoot out the top of my head. I climbed and climbed and climbed, until everything came falling down so fast I almost passed out. As Rosa strokes my arm, the same feeling begins.

► ► ►

I wake up from a nightmare and tiptoe down to the kitchen for a glass of water. It's past midnight and the entire house is quiet. As I walk through the breakfast nook, I see that someone's left a light on in the den. Careful not to let the floorboards creak, I enter. Frank and Susie are on the couch. Susie's skirt is pushed up around her waist, and Frank's hands are under her blouse. I freeze. I know I should turn around and run back to my room, but I can't stop watching. I've always like Frank until now, or at least didn't mind him, and I can't quite believe that he would do such a thing.

Suddenly, Susie bolts upright, pushing Frank off of her. "Hey, Jeannie," she says. "Have a bad dream?"

I nod, still staring at Frank. He won't look at me.

"I'm sorry, sweetie," Susie says. "Why don't I take you back up to bed?"

"Suz —," Frank calls as she slips from the couch and puts an arm around me.

"I won't be two minutes," she reassures him.

In my room, she tucks me in and sits on the bed beside me. "You okay?" she asks.

I nod and close my eyes, hoping to fall right to sleep. "Susie," I say, "can I ask you something?"

"Uh-huh."

"Why did you let him do that?"

"Do what?"

"You know. What you were doing. In the den."

"Oh." She smoothes my hair away from my forehead and presses in close to my ear. "Cuz I like it."

"You do?"

"Uh-huh. You will, too. One day."

I try to take this in but can't believe it. "You mean he wasn't hurting you?"

"No." She sits up and looks at me. "Is that what you're so worried about?"

"Yeah," I whisper.

"Oh, sweetie," she says. "No, Frank would never hurt me."

"Okay." I manage to keep my eyes closed long enough for Susie to leave but stay awake long after I hear the front door close and Frank go down into the basement to bed.

▸ ▸ ▸

Safely tucked behind the auditorium, I push the sleeve of Rosa's sweater over her arm and run my fingers along the inside of her elbow. She shivers and closes her eyes. "Rosa?" I ask. "Are we going to have to do this with boys one day?"

She looks at me and crinkles her nose. "God. I hope not."

"Yeah," I say. "Me, too."

Best Bandanna

Tanya Davis

That first day, smitten, as you talked about bear safety, leaning on your shovel, squinting at us. At dinner you belched and laughed uninhibited, your head thrown back like wild sex; I was overtaken.

There was free beer for the entire camp that first night, and then joints, and then kitchen raids, and then me and you in a tent with liquor on our breath and not enough blankets. I was so bold as to kiss your cold cheek that night, and your earlobe, your jawline. You laughed: I fell in love with you. Girlish and lusty love; too-quick, dangerous love.

The morning was damp, cold and early; breakfast was over by the time I got there. I thought about you every time I put a tree in the ground and all week, every time I put a tree in the ground, I thought about you.

Our first night off we hit the closest bar in the closest town and you got so drunk someone had to walk you back to the hotel. I put down my glass and stumbled home with you. It was cold up there and we stopped to hug for warmth against a brick wall, because we were curious, because that's where drunk girls everywhere stop to hug. The kiss was hard and dramatic, tongues exploring mouths and teeth and stamina, your strong body pressed to mine, your cunt coming down firm along my thigh.

We made it to the lobby after a few of these stops, each one ending abruptly with a, "we can't do this," and a drunken disclaimer on your behalf. You ducked quickly then into a room of sleeping treeplanters; I wandered the halls awhile, smug to think of you lying there, thinking of me.

The next day we set up a new camp and I fucked you over and over in my head. The day after that we got back to work and every day after that I loved you more. I memorized the freckles on your face that summer and gave you my best bandanna, so I might get closer to the hairs on your head. On good nights you invited me into your tent to sleep beside you, when the fire died down, when no one else was looking. I tickled your back and you sighed; I had never been so turned on and you said, "this is better than sex." I tickled most of your body and you moaned and I never told you what you felt like to my fingertips, never told you that this was love for me. We slept soundly and close together on these nights. Your dog was in there, too.

Only one time you whispered outside of my tent to come in, threw your weight over me and came at my mouth like it was water and you'd been walking for days without any. You tasted my pussy, pushing my legs apart and burying your face between them, breathing hard and flicking harder until I came, shuddering, in your mouth. You told me you loved to do that; you told me that you couldn't let me give it back to you. And so we slept.

That was the only night my tent had you, my blankets held you, the night the spiders in my corners spun their webs above us and you stayed until the morning warned you off, until the earliest birds chirped.

This was the summer I accepted love at your convenience, following your cocked eyebrow into empty bathrooms and dark corners, past unsuspecting boys gathered at pool tables, past your fellow supervisors, who might have known but never said anything. It was the summer that I watched you sleep, gave you my shoulder on long bus rides. It was innocent and sexy and secretive; it was tortured and I loved you anyway.

These are fragments from a summer that showed me lust was real and breathtaking, showed me that I could love a woman and she could break my heart, quietly, against a brick wall that never crumbled, because falling bricks draw too much attention and no one could ever know.

This was the summer that you left a week early, before the last tree was planted. I got back to camp at the end of the day and found your handwriting on my tent floor, your bandanna on my pillow. You left me a note, not even a letter. You left me without a conversation or a kiss. This was the first time I loved a woman, completely. It was the last time I saw you.

First

N.M. Maro

I will never forget my first kiss. Well, technically, it was my second, but my *first* first was slobbery and with a boy, and although that was an interesting scenario, I prefer to boldly proclaim that I was born lesbian (which I was) and that my first kiss was experienced with a dashing soft butch or perhaps a striking androgynous gal, which it *almost* was.

I met Beckie at my first place of employment, a huge corporation that requires its workers to don blue polos and scratchy tan khakis. Needless to say, I did not win Beckie over with a fabulous clothing ensemble. Beckie, too, fell victim to uniformity, but there was always something different about her, something brilliantly intriguing, sexy, and downright stimulating. Perhaps it was her piercing blue eyes that lit up when we spoke, her big infectious laugh . . . or the way she sold her appliances. Beckie worked in refrigerators, situated directly across from the media department, my treasured section, and I delighted in our proximity. I had the perfect view: Beckie, Rebecca, Becca.

I was an eleventh grader then, and I would write our initials in the margins of my notebooks to pass time during an excruciating math class. I'd configure my own equations, such as "Becca O + Nicole M = sheer happiness," and in government class, my margin notes would get political and ecological: *Dyke Love Will Save The Planet.*

Now, *I* knew what I was, but frighteningly I did not even know if my beloved Rebecca was Sapphic. Then I overheard a burly guy from electronics bust out in the break room, "You know big Beckie from fridges?" – Beckie stood a dashing five feet, ten inches – "I heard she dates a five-foot-tall Asian dude! He's from Montana." I was utterly and completely crushed. But considering the source, I set out to find out for myself.

Blessedly, fate was on my side. As I hadn't yet mustered up the courage to speak with Beckie, much less inquire of her sexual orientation and relationship status, I was lucky enough to be informed by the source herself.

In the middle of snatching a DMX CD for a loyal customer, I felt a gentle yet confident tap on my shoulder. I turned around to face the sight of all sights, the beauty of all beauties – Rebecca.

"I'm gonna take a cig break," she said. "Wanna join me?"

Now, I detest cigarettes, but at that point in my life, my requirements for potential wives were slim to nil. I fervently believed that if Beckie smoked, it would be enticing, as opposed to smelly and life-threatening. I graciously accepted her invitation.

What happened next was momentous. No, we didn't kiss. That comes much later. What *did* happen involved Beckie coming out as bisexual, not gay, so that basically put my U-haul plan on hold. But I was not particular at that point in my life, so half-gay counted in my book. As I sat on the cement stoop inhaling nicotine and that sweet Rebecca smell, I felt so good, so sure of everything. I took a chance and asked Beckie to an upcoming lesbian folk concert, and she said yes. I envisioned the perfect date: Ferron, mocha lattés, and then a mega-making-out session, my first lesbian experience, the one that would crown me a bona-fide sister of the woodlands.

Okay. So it didn't happen at all like that. Instead, we went and saw Ferron, and I got to enjoy the appreciative looks from older Sapphic souls and the illusion that Beckie and I were in a loving, lezzie relationship. We didn't hold hands, but our thighs did touch on one occasion during the concert, and she gave me a stick of Juicy Fruit, which I hate but immediately began to adore. (Six years later and the wrapper remains laminated in a photo album.) Beckie poked fun at the music and made numerous remarks that could have indicated she was having a lousy time.

"Look at these women! I have totally counted seventy-six mullets." (Gorgeous laugh.) "Nicole, I think you brought me to Geriatric Dyke-Land!" (Playful jab that sent chills up my spine.)

Beckie didn't enjoy the music and we didn't go for mocha lattés after the show; instead, we grabbed slices of Oreo pie at Denny's. But we did go to her place after that. Do you think we did it, Chastity Bono-style, to the music of the Indigo Girls, on silky lavender sheets with labrys insignia? Think again. Instead, Beckie took me to her tiny, one-bedroom apartment and sang songs she had written, while accompanying herself on acoustic guitar. Then she took me home. Although I must admit that evening was a bit of a letdown, it was the closest to heaven I'd been yet.

Many months passed, and it was finally time to say goodbye to everything

I had ever known, to Beckie and Best Buy and Mom and friends. It was time to go away to college. The night before leaving, I drove over to Beckie's with a plan I so longed to make happen. I would seduce her and leave for college a card-carrying member of the softball league, humming Jill Sobule and busting out my pride rings. And seduce her I did, just not exactly successfully.

What it really came down to was pleading and begging Beckie to kiss me. She thought the whole thing was hilarious and almost didn't comply. She burst out, "Oh my God! I'm not . . . I wasn't . . . expecting this!" (Raucous laughter that was starting to sound obnoxious.) "I gotta get some water with lemon!" So Becca cleaned her pallet and made her breath all citrusy and I thrust myself upon her. It lasted a whopping twenty-one seconds. It was sloppy, wet, but felt refreshingly good, right, and my heart danced.

When it was over, Beckie gazed at me intently. "With some practice, you'll get the hang of it. You know, Nicole, that was like kissing my sister. I'm twenty-three and you're seventeen and I couldn't even, like, buy you a beer."

So I moved on to college and many, many more firsts, another Becky (that's right, but with a "Y" this time), and incredibly true adventures of lesbiandom. But I'll never forget that first kiss. It wasn't great, but it was good enough for me.

Muna Who Lives in a Church

Helena Settimana

Muna, who lives in a church adjacent to my home, stands in the darkened doorway while I walk from work in the fog. I must pass her to get to my place. I walk with my head down. As I turn the corner, I see her there in the shadow, obscured by the yellow mist which slinks around her waist. The streetlamps are haloed by the dampness in the air.

I've seen her from the window of her flat looking out over the roof-tops and then down at me in my garden. Dark. Desert-dark. She has coiled hair, thick corkscrews of it. She looks tall, with small breasts, a big ass on powerful thighs. One time she drew her fingers between her legs, pushed her pussy at me. I blinked and ran into my house like a frightened rabbit. I rode my own hand remembering the shock of her and then crept outside again to see if she was still there, watching, beckoning. How could she see through me like that?

And so I'm hurrying home in the darkness of a December evening, when I see her. Her hair is a riot in the damp. I try to rush past, half-hoping she'll call to me while dreading that she will. And Muna who lives in a church calls out, "'ave you got a Rizla, love?" and I pause, and then stop, heart pounding and ask, "What?" and she says it again. "A Rizla. A rolly. A paper?" She knows I've got one, because she's seen me fish Drum from a packet in my pocket. She must have seen this, looking down on me sunning, smoking in the garden. She pulls out a plastic pouch in which I expect to see shag, but it's not. She rolls the biggest number I've ever seen with one hand while barely dropping me from her sight. She inhales. "Want some?" She holds it out, and I'm a step closer to her until our fingertips touch. I'm fretful, and she asks what I'm scared of. Nothing. Nothing. Not scared of anything, not scared at all. I learn her name.

Muna, who lives in a church, takes my hand and leads me across the cobbles, the broken pavement before the church; Muna pushes the grand gothic doors open; Muna mounts the stairs with me, passes her spliff back, pulls my hand in hers, which is strong. She's acting with such confidence I feel a bit like a mouse before a cobra. This can't be happening. But it is.

There are big, arched windows in the clerestory space where she lives. Prayer rugs, paradise garden rugs are on the floor, on the brick walls. The ceiling vaults above my head. Her flat overlooks the tiled roofs and chimney pots of the grey neighborhood. There's a light on in my back garden and I see what I already know. The paper is burning my fingers while I'm inhaling and coughing and putting my bag down so I can unbutton my coat and begin on my shirt, when she steps in and helps me out, not even talking, not telling me she thinks I'm hot but showing me with her lips which grasp my earlobe and her tongue which trails delicately from my ear to my mouth. Teeth, her teeth pluck at my skin, begin to unbutton my shirt near the navel and my legs are buckling under me. I think I might pass out.

Muna is naked in her church – in her sanctuary, with a view of the blurry crescent moon through the elder tree in my garden. There is a ring around the moon. The ground below blanketed with mist. Muna demands a tithe of adoration be paid before I get my reward. I think I will die of the unbelievable good fortune of walking into this woman's arms, into this woman's bed or at least the futon before the window.

There are steel rings through her nipples. There is a steel ring through her nose. Her hair smells like Lush and dope and patchouli.

Putting my face between her legs is not alien, though she's bearded and thick there, hair in extravagant abundance, glossy and fragrant. Her slit, her clit show dimly through the thatch. But Muna is high and excited and flushed with the triumph of her conquest. My fingers find her heat and her loosening hole, plumb her insides, stroke her wee hardness until she grasps my wrist with her vise-grip hands and tells me to stop. Stop now. *Please, stop.*

I'm half-undressed. My shirttails hang out. She has slipped her fingers into the fly of my trousers, rolled down the waist, run her fingers under the scalloped edge of my panties, through the sparse hair, dipped herself into me and licked my juice from her hand. I pull off my pants, step out of their heap on the floor and fall into her. She tears at my breasts, teeth, tongue. I ride her thigh for what seems a delicious forever, growing wetter and more oblivious with each fevered stroke of my gash over the fine hair of her leg. It scrapes me on the forward stroke, like a cat's tongue. And so I come, un-touched, uninvaded, hotter than asphalt in July, drizzling spent desire.

We sleep, both of us, jumbled on the futon until the first light of day begins to brighten the pea-soup sky. There are faint hints of pink and yel-low and baby blue behind the grey-white. She makes coffee and small talk and I realize it's time to go back to work. Time to go home, feed the cat, dress in a different costume and begin my day all over again. Tonight, when I walk home, I'll push through the doors of the church, ascend the stairs, and *'allelujah*, seek another glimpse of heaven.

Flirt

Denise Nico Leto

We're having a skin conversation. Only, she doesn't know it. Sitting in the restaurant, gazing at her lips, I can forgive the food we are eating that looks like her – plum and wildly herbed. I am wedded to a woman with a saffron lair. She sets delicate spiders free in the yellow light of dusk. She eats only the ones she loves. I am the one she loves. I am having dinner with a woman to whom I am not married. She is lovelier than what is forgiven. I only need her star for a day. She is married to a man with a silver earring and has three kids who live in a house with a red living room. I have been in that living room. I swoon in the red, the purple of her taste. The kids play. The husband stares into the brightly colored walls looking for a safe haven. This is the family design and the pattern is out of my hands.

She is a mosaicist. She breaks things and puts them back together in beauty. I want her to break me, to put me back together so that I don't recognize myself. I could be a fountain, say, or a bench. Maybe a terracotta pot with many colored tiles. A hot plate. A mirror. I don't care. We speak of our lives in code. I am a perfect cipher. I understand things she doesn't say. I caress her words with my hands. When I catch her eye, she streaks across the firmament. When I touch her hips in my mind, water falls from every curve. There is a body flood. She floats in second grace, third, fourth. Down river. Up river. All the way there and back. But she is really just telling me about her day. The jewelry store she went to. The rose gold ring she bought. She extends her hand to show me the band. It is a pink Saturn ring and I am Jupiter. Get me away from here. Far, far away.

It is her fiftieth birthday. I wait to call. I am always waiting. No one knows the tenure of my wait. It is permanent; a stirring desire in luminous fixity. No one can replace me because I am not really there. She notices our friendship. It registers with nobility. But I am ignoble. I imagine her wet and nude in a sauna. I walk around her body; I smell the damp aroma.

She is wine from carved wood barrels. She is loose steam escaping from the window. When we kiss in my mind she brings out the boy in me. We have sex in movie theaters. I take her to the back aisle. Turn her face toward me. Kiss her to intermission. Spread her legs in the seat next to mine, stretch my hand down her silk pants to better silk. To rain's silk. I sneak down in my chair. I kiss her belly heat; I take her pussy in my mouth. The red, the purple – Catherine Deneuve, Chiara Mastroianni, Lorraine Bracco – the cinematic coming. She is the afterstorm. The dripping trees, the steaming puddles, the dewy sidewalk, the husky granules of dawn. The End.

I am fucked. I send her a card about the film. I speak of the intellectual dilemma of irresolution. She responds in kind. I go to her studio for lunch. It is drafty. There are sharp bits of tesserae everywhere. Sweep them up, glue them all together, and I would give them my shirt. Warm them like lambs. Feed them fresh grass. Give them a home. What am I talking about? Nips of tile. That is all. Anything she touches animates. My lover thinks I am feverish. She feels my forehead. I tell her all I can think about is the woman who makes mosaics. She puts her arms around my entire body and I cry. She licks my tears. I tell her I am lucky. She licks my tears. Here I am, with her: somewhere. There I am with the lady of aisles, of waiting: nowhere. I am touched like an apricot. I cannot be preserved. She sends me to therapy. I speak in dreams. In one, I am a lion who reads books with her paws. I send out my cubs for takeout. They bring back Fortune Cookies that say, "You will be fortuitous in business." In another, I am reading Edith Wharton on a raft in the Mediterranean; there are a million bits of shattered tile on the shore instead of sand. I walk through them and my feet bleed. My flowing blood becomes the grout. The random bits of tile take shape, but I can recognize no shape. I wake up.

I begin to compile a list of poetry. Love poems I will read in her absence. I devour them. They seem so real. Each page is vital nourishment. I am otherwise famished. Desire shapes me as wind shapes sand: relentless, beautiful, eroding. My therapist tells me sexual desire is. . . . I don't understand a word she says. I take the mosaicist out to dinner. We have an appetizer of sea urchin and cucumber. We have tall glasses of wine. I surrender. I stand on the table and wave a white flag. She smiles and her teeth are hard candies. I bend toward her and lick them. One is dark cherry. One is mint. One is chocolate. One is coffee. One is butterscotch. I forget the end of conflict. She forgets the beginning of masks. I touch her breast. God, let me suck it. Let her into my mouth. The mouth of my mouth takes her in. We are in my car now. A small economy. I suck her kaleidoscope nipple. Enter her plum-lit pussy. Fuck her till the curtain comes down.

Bugger

Wickie Stamps

BUG (BUG) N. I. ANY INSECT OR INSECT-LIKE INVERTEBRATE.*
I've always identified with things that showed up when not wanted. Like bugs. I too was misplaced, dislocated. I bugged people, made them squirm. With twigs in my unruly hair, or my nose in a book I was too boyish, too smart, too grubby — never girl enough for anyone. My looks and ways snuck up on people. Scared them. Scattered them.

Now I am sentenced to this freakish ghetto called San Francisco with other bugs — as scary and grubby as me.

BUGGER (BUG'ER) N. I. SODOMITE.
I edit a magazine for the macho gay male. Each day I enter a world of big-dicked men where images of sweat, piss, and cum are scattered over my desk.

I hang up some pictures of young Euroboys on the wall in front of my desk.

"I know who you think those boys are," my co-worker said, peering close at the fey boys. "You think they are young boy dykes, don't you?" he said.

"You're right," I admitted.

BUGGER (BUG'ER) N. 2. A FELLOW, LAD, OR CHILD, OFTEN USED AFFECTIONATELY.
Night after night I ride my motorcycle to the clubs and cruise young tranny boys. They run in boy packs keeping the exclusive company of other boys. I lean back into the bar's shadows and watch them — young, faggish, and pretty. I obsess about taking one of these young boys into the bathroom and fucking him in the ass. These thoughts gnaw at my mind, distract me from my work.

I study the ass of the slim-hipped boy dyke walking a few strides in front of me. I imagine sliding my hand up her ass, fucking her thin body, forcing him to come.

"Do you like getting fucked in the ass?" I say. We wander through the Castro. With his razor short haircut, she's — sometimes "he" as fits her/his fancy — is cruised by the chicken hawks passing by. I catch her prissy smirk in the reflection of the glass where the movie *Female Perversions* is advertised.

"Sure," he says easily without missing a stride. I reach out and run my hand over her buzz cut. "It's been a while," she adds.

During sex, she asks me not to fuck her on her back; she doesn't like feeling like a girl. So I turn her over, pull her up on her knees, and fuck her from behind. I am careful not to let her feel like a girl. As she rides my cock, face down on the sheets, ass up, I slide my fingers, first one then two, into her ass. She hisses that she hates me. With my cock deep in her cunt she shoves her ass back onto my fingers and comes. Her hair is damp, eyes closed. She whimpers.

BUG (BUG) N. 2. A VIRUS.
He lies in my bed, resting. Something she says she needs to do a lot as he says he is ill. Ill with a sickness I cannot stop, cannot control, do not understand. No one knows the cause — or the cure. She is chronically fatigued. I've seen the exhaustion creep over him, like a plague — silent, relentless, determined.

I see his illness after I have fucked her hard, after she has broken out in a cold sweat. With my cock still in her, he rests her damp forehead on my shoulder. I hold him, stroke his damp hair, and run my warm hands down her cool back. I notice her pallor and think of the cancer patients I've known, men and women whose internal lights grow dim, energy dissipating. Pale as a wax candle, deepening to grey. She rests on me, heavy now, a dead weight. I kiss the top of her head, smooth her boyish bangs.

BUG (BUG) SLANG. TO ANNOY. TO IRRITATE.
Her illness — and her complaining — bugs me, creates waves around my affection for her.

I am bugged — no, I am angered — by her illness and the selfishness that swarms around her, both taking her from me without warning. At its own whim. The selfishness, that is increasingly predictable, consistent, and now inseparable from her illness.

I fight with her. I accuse her of being selfish and self-centered. I lash out at her for her obsessive need to take care of herself. I lecture her and tell her that she is not the only one who exists between us, that she is not the only one who has problems. I go on and on about how lonely I feel and how I will not again nor ever be consumed by a woman. She sits up in her sick bed, wraps a blanket around her thin shoulders, wearily puts on her wire-rimmed glasses as fragile as she and, suddenly, she is back. Listening to me. Connecting. Mine. Momentarily.

She lies down again, begins complaining. My lips curl in disgust. I am bugged by *my* own exhaustion. I am pestered now by *my* desire to be fucked – by a tranny boy, younger than me. One less tired – and with fewer troubles.

BUG (BUG) 6. *SLANG.* A. A PERSON WHO HAS A GREAT ENTHUSIASM FOR SOMETHING; A FAN; A HOBBYIST. B. AN OBSESSION.

I stare out my office windows onto Market by Castro, scanning for young tranny boys who might be willing to go into the public bathroom across the way and let me suck their cock – or they mine. I take a break and walk into the Castro looking into the eyes of the young dykes and trannys who pass me by, wondering which one will take me into the too-few alleys during the too-bright daylight and fuck me in the ass. Or will it be me who takes them in the twenty-five-cent-for-ten-minute toilet right across the street?

Black Harley, White Sheets

Bronwyn Scanlon

It ends in a bed but starts on a road. The seduction factor is, of course, her motorcycle. The light spills all over the aluminum and chrome and breaks in shards across the exhaust pipes and dual-fishtail mufflers. The warm hum of the engine, which vibrates as she cocks her long leg before throwing it over the body. Her fingers curl tight about rubber grips.

Right from the beginning, there is a feel, a physicality, I can get lost in.

She is a girl with anarchic energy to burn and I am a girl with a short supply of that kind of fuel. And I am still young enough to mistake her language of clamps and clutch levers, stick shifts and chains, her talk of the material world as openness. I haven't yet learned to look for stories within stories. I have just broken up with my girlfriend and from my black room I am drawn to her well-mounted light. I proceed with blind faith.

The first time I see her, she is pulling her red helmet from her head and running her hand through her dark hair. From a street café, I watch her take off her leather jacket, gloves, chaps. A slow sidewalk striptease. And as she passes my table, I tell her I love her machine. She looks back at the rear fender of her Harley with its retro '40s tombstone taillight and sixteen-inch laced wheels, then turns toward me. I pull back the chair for her, patting the wood of the seat.

Her shirt gapes as she puts down her gear. Black lace, straps, skin. A freckle close to her cleavage. She places her hands on the table like stray tools. And I watch her cast her gaze across my shoulders, breasts, lap, like she is inspecting angles on a chassis. When she looks at me, I know what she wants.

A short while later, we ride towards her apartment, cruising along a stretch of road winding about the coastline. Blue waves crash white against massive slick rocks. My thighs press against her hips. We lean into curves and accelerate into open spaces. Her crazy smell roaring across my face, hair.

Inside, she becomes an acrobat. Dragging me across tables and chairs. Pushing me against walls, my calves on her shoulders. My butt resting on her forearms. Her mouth, tongue attacking me from every angle. Tearing away our clothes with each maneuver. Till finally, sprawled on the floor, she touches me, for the first time. The splay of her fingers hard against my back. A kiss like a lock. Then the slow turning wheel of our limbs, our bodies, fitting into each other. The graze of teeth. The shine of sweat. And a precision, a perfect timing I do not expect.

After, warm water funnels between our breasts, bellies, thighs. Her face buried against the soft wet skin of my neck. My shoulders hard against the tiles. She takes me again. Cascade of water. My knees wrapped about her. Her quick joke about soap. My teeth in her arm. The clear fall of water.

▸ ▸ ▸

I fall in love with kamikaze speed. Her muscle love and bottles of red wine lubricate everything. You are my dreamgirl, she says, and I fall into the slipstream of long nights, long rides, and hours of reckless conversation. On one of these nights, I learn about her ex-lover. The one that hasn't let go. Her name just hangs in the air, like something left out to dry. Something the natural elements will take care of. I recall now the name punctuated many of her stories, but at the time it seemed insubstantial. Like a breeze could carry it away.

Nothing could impede our love motion.

Then one Friday night, she doesn't call. Just like that. The silence of my phone, deafening. I pace about the rooms of my apartment resisting my collision with destiny. Struck by the depth of my feeling. I lie on the floor listening to rain on the roof. The windows smeared with water, darkness. It is well after midnight when I finally fall asleep.

The next morning, one of her male friends calls me. He says she has been in an accident.

Something upset her. She shouldn't have been on her bike.

He won't say what. Won't tell me what had driven my new love into a thunderstorm and across to the other side of the city. Won't say what had made her forget me. Instead, he reads out a ward number and reassures me that everything will be okay.

I have to wait for answers.

▸ ▸ ▸

Her recovery is long. Six weeks in a rehabilitation hospital. "Dykes meet institution" throws up all kinds of challenges. We have to be creative. The white crisp uniforms and blue cotton screens note how regularly I visit. Note what a loyal "friend" I am. The way I arrive with armfuls of tiger lilies, books, and silk boxer shorts. The way I stay by her bed till I am asked to leave.

Finally, her leg is lowered. The plaster removed. Her wrist, suddenly mobile. She tells stories about the policewoman she met while lying on the road. The shape of her ankles. The gravel in her voice. And how her uniform buttons pulled apart under the duress of her breasts. The tension between us builds. The metal bed, the clean sheets. The curtain walls we pull about us. My hand slipping across her thigh, stroking her. The staff instinctively retreating.

Her three small words breathed into my ear as her back arches.

It is later, the same night that her ex-girlfriend appears by the bed. An apparition in blue jeans and a Mona Lisa smile. I leave them alone. But from the doorway I hear the girl speak.

I've left her. I want you back.

And, from the doorway, I watch the kiss of life. On the same white sheets I witness the resurrection of their relationship. And watch my world turn. Again.

Play It Again, Sam

Stephanie Schroeder

I'm a gold-star lesbian. I've never had sex with a man. For years I bought into that radical feminist junk about how to have equal and "politically correct" lesbian sex: I was doing the side-by-side, you take your turn, and I'll take mine, no penetration, vanilla thing forever. Well, honey, Andrea Dworkin's got a boyfriend, Catherine MacKinnon is married, and Anne Koedt, the woman who told me I couldn't possibly have a vaginal orgasm, who knows where the hell she is? And, baby, you know what? They were *all* wrong. Cock — women's cock, that is — it's a great thing.

So, tired of not getting what I really wanted, I decided to go out and get me some, I even bought it. My first experience was not all that long ago. I met this hot butch online. You know — the PlanetOut phenomena of the late '90s — lesbian online dating mania. One early Monday morning, I opened my email and found a short note from her saying hello. So I checked out her profile, she seemed the perfect butch: singing in her car to '80s music, volunteering in the community, a solid job and graduate school, very handsome with a devilish smile. What more could a girl possibly want? Well, maybe she would have a strap-on . . . now, that would be perfect.

So I wrote back to her and asked, "Do you own your cock? Because my friend and I were talking the other day and she said that it's one thing for just any lesbian to strap on a dildo and quite another for a butch to own her cock. *So*, I want to know, do you own your cock?" And the answer was exactly what I was looking for: yep, she did, but she told me that if she and I were going to fuck, I would have to bring my own. Cock, that is.

So how does a vanilla lesbian go about buying a dildo? I was *not* going into the Pink Pussycat, my first New York encounter with sex toys over ten years ago. I would *not* go face-to-face with a sex shop salesperson. So, I went the anonymous route and went on Toys in Babeland's website to check out all their dildos. I read the voluminous information about silicone, reasons for various shapes and sizes, the place of dildos in our history. Then I cruised the specimens. I picked out "Bogart," who was in the famous company of Bond and Brando. She was not too long nor too thick for my first time. Bogart was the one, my first cock for my first butch fuck. She was purple, too

"Purple?" my butch exclaimed, when I told her it just *had* to be purple; no flesh-colored, penis-type cock for me. "You gotta be fuckin' kiddin' me," she said. "But hey, it's your cock." She probably thought I must be a crazy and silly little inexperienced girl from the Midwest. My butch and I talked about latex and I scored some blue gloves from the café downstairs from where I worked. "I see a color scheme going on here," my butch replied, ribbing me via email just hours before our appointed meeting.

It was at the the Liberty Inn, a pay-by-the-hour motel in the meatpacking district. She was not as tall as I had expected, but wide enough for my taste. The texture of her skin was magnificent and she tasted fresh and clean. She was handsome and beautiful at the same time, a butch tool for femme pleasure. I am, of course, talking about both the butch and the cock. The feeling of Bogart sliding into my lubed cunt and being pushed and thrust into me by a big hunk of a woman in a tight t-shirt and boxers, with Bogart hard and at the ready peeking out of her fly, was all I needed. That night changed me and my sex life forever.

After that, I began sucking cock, masturbating with them, and getting fucked by butches packing cocks. I became an expert: the different sizes, the textures, the smells, the various colors, length and girth; which ones were good for packing, which ones were not.

I wrote all about cock – both theoretically and erotically. But you know, it's all in the presentation. My butch – and the cock – were fierce that night, all posture and pose and stance and thrust.

Like I said, it's all in the presentation. Cock. I love it. I want it, I need it. Women packin' it, that is!

My Fantasy is Dead

Midgett

The honeymoon is over. My fantasy is dead.

The doorbell rings. Our eyes meet. She is five-foot-nine, with a 170-pound frame of solid muscle. Her brownness is a mixture of cinnamon and copper. Sue has invited me to dinner, and invited her friend Sharon too. After she steps inside, Sharon takes off her backpack, then her jacket and sweater. Her large muscles are exposed. She weares a white T-shirt, which accentuates her brown skin. I am breathless when she looks at me, her brown eyes full and dancing.

We sit down to eat. Sharon and I sit close, our eyes meet briefly: I stare at her. She avoids my gaze. I am in love.

Dinner finished, dishes washed, we continue talking. I want to go home. I want to take her with me. I want her. My pussy aches, throbs. I ask Sharon if she could give me a ride home. When she says, "yes," my heart starts to pound so fast and loud, I worry they can hear it beating.

Sharon and I say goodnight to Sue and leave together. I can't believe I have her all to myself. Outside, I proposition her, our arms linked together. Inside her car, the fantasy begins. I am on cloud nine. She drives with both hands on the steering wheel. I can't keep my arms off of her. I kiss her ears, lips and cheeks while caressing her thighs. I am in heat.

She parks the car; I go inside and slip on a sheer black negligee. I sit in the living room, near the front door, in anticipation, waiting for the doorbell to ring.

When it does I open the door, feeling faint. I fling my arms around her neck and push her against the wall. She embraces my waist with such force she cuts off my breath for a moment. She pulls her body against mine, and slowly grinds her pelvis against my pussy. Heat rises between our legs. No words are necessary. I lead her to the bedroom. Lips, bodies, pussies become one.

We marry, her children move in. The honeymoon is over. My fantasy is dead.

She

Jolie du Pré

My mink throw was a gift to me, from me, for becoming the first female African American partner at the company. She pulls it out and spreads it on the middle of my living room floor. We have removed our clothes and tonight I lay on its mahogany fur, naked, with my wrist bound in front of my stomach.

"You want some of that cat?" she says.

She kneels on top of me as I lay between her taut, black thighs. My eyes focus on her firm ass and hairy pussy. "Yes," I say. "Give it to me." I lift my upper body, straining to catch her bush with my mouth.

She shoots me a look. "When I tell you, bitch."

I lower myself down, staring at her cunt, wanting it and waiting.

"Now," she says. She sits on my face. I'm smothered in the sodden mass of her musk. I burrow in it, taste it and inhale it. "Enough," she says, and she lifts herself from my face. I wait until she gives it to me again.

At work, the following morning, I'm in my office in a meeting. My cell phone is on the desk. It rings and I pick it up. "Hello," I say.

"Can you smell it?" That's all she says.

I can smell it. I can smell it while I sit in my office, staring at a bunch of white men staring at me. I can smell it, and I almost forget what I'm supposed to say to them.

At home, after work, I walk into my bedroom and notice that my black latex dress is laid out on my bed and that my black stilettos are at the foot of it. There's a note. "Put these on."

I listen and look around for her, but I don't see or hear her. I take off my clothes and shoes and squeeze into the latex. Then I slip on the stilettos.

"Don't move," a voice says. She's in there with me, behind me. "Get on your knees," she says. And I do.

She places a blindfold over my eyes and cuffs my hands behind my back. She leaves me there. My thoughts turn within. I think about the night I met her, at the club.

In that room, she stood there. Everywhere I went, she followed me with her eyes. She walked up to me, the only other black in the room, and said, "Get me a drink." I didn't know her and she didn't know me. But she told me to get her a drink, and I did.

Later, at her house, she placed me face down on her bed, my wrists and ankles tied. She reached into a chest, removed a paddle, and whacked my bare bottom until I cried out in pain.

"Come back at six tomorrow," she said.

"Can't I come later?" I asked. "I have a meeting at six."

"No," she said. "I said six. Don't disappoint me."

I remember staring at a bunch of papers while at work, the day after she spanked me, the same day she wanted me to meet her at six, and feeling the pain lingering on my ass. Glorious.

I could have blown her off and attended the meeting. I could have saved myself the trouble of having to reschedule. I could have. But I didn't.

The Souvenir

Tawanna Sullivan

It happened the night of Rita's birthday party. After everyone else left, I stuck around to help her clean up. We didn't get through until about four a.m. Rita offered to let me stay on the sofa, but I'm not afraid to catch the subway at night.

I caught the P local at the Reed Street Station. It was a cold five-minute wait for the train, but I got an entire subway car to myself. At least, for about the first three stops. Then, at Forest Station, this dark chocolate beauty stepped in. She had a short, curly brown afro with honey-blonde streaks and her breasts strained against a low cut, sheer blouse. I lowered my gaze to her thigh-high, black leather boots, which ended at the hem of her mini-skirt.

I was just starting to admire the perfect curve of her ass when another woman walked in after her. It was obvious they were a couple. Wearing black dress pants and a Polo shirt, the girlfriend looked like she had stepped out of the pages of GQ.

Now, with all the space available, these two sat directly in front of me. Honey was practically sitting in her girl's lap. They were whispering and stealing peeks at me, but I was determined to ignore them. I had totally blocked them out, until a low, sensuous purr caught my attention. GQ had a hand up Honey's blouse and was kissing her neck. The moans were coming from Honey. She was biting her lower lip but looking straight at me.

Suddenly, Honey's breasts were fully exposed and freely swaying with the movement of the train. Turning her back to me, Honey straddled GQ's legs and began rubbing against her. GQ pushed up the mini-skirt, revealing a supple booty barely contained in a black thong. "Yes, baby, fill me up," Honey said, her moans interrupted by little cries of pleasure.

My nipples were throbbing and my pussy was a damn waterfall. I wanted to be GQ. I could just imagine pushing the thong aside and my fingers being sucked in by Honey's pussy. I'd rub her clit with my thumb while tickling her g-spot and nibble on her nipples as she bucked against me.

I wanted to cross the aisle and plant little kisses all over Honey's back. My tongue would trace the contours of her spine and delve into the cleft of her ass. Instead, I rocked back and forth, savoring the sensation of my lips sliding against my clit.

Honey slid off of GQ's fingers and nearly lost her balance as she sat on the bench. GQ got down on her knees. Draping a leg over each shoulder, she buried her face in Honey's pussy.

Bracing herself, Honey winked at me. "That's right, baby. Suck it. Isn't it juicy?" She began writhing and twisting, but her eyes never left mine. "I'm ready to come for you, baby. Just for you—" Suddenly, she arched her back and her gasps and screams echoed throughout the car, empty except for us three.

GQ immediately stood up and gathered Honey in her arms. They cuddled and kissed for a moment and then Honey started dressing. My pussy was quivering. All my clit needed was one good stroke.

When the train pulled into the Liberty Street Station, they rose out of their seats. Honey wriggled out of her cum-soaked thong and dropped it in my lap on her way out.

A souvenir that was for keeps.

Kate's Taste of Fame

Sarah Ellen

Kate entered the bar and looked around for a suitable table. Thankfully there were plenty to choose from despite it being the lunch hour. She glanced at her watch, relieved to find she still had plenty of time. Time in which to better her composure before she had to meet Jan this afternoon. She would be calm but firm.

She bought a drink at the bar and chose a table along the periphery of the room, sensing she might need the seclusion it offered. Despite her well-planned strategy, heaven only knew how Jan was going to react to the decision she'd made.

Feeling conspicuous, she reached into her bag and pulled out a magazine, gazing at the list of contents. Eagerly she found the page she sought, a full-length feature on her favorite American actress, Krista Starbright, rumoured to be gay and promoting her latest film. She stared at the beautiful photos, losing herself in her flights of ridiculous fancy, as Jan called them.

Kate sighed. She hated it when Jan mocked her. What was so wrong with daydreaming once in a while? Was she worried that Kate's imaginary lovers would spur her into someone else's bed? Or was it the age gap between them that made her so insecure?

The sound of people approaching made her look up, but it was just a group of strangers taking seats at the bar nearby, so she returned to her magazine.

She took a sip from her glass and glanced at the group next to her. There were four of them: two men, large and muscle-bound, and two women who seemed tiny next to them. Oddly, the men appeared uneasy in their surroundings – anxious and almost overprotective. Perhaps they were ultra possessive, Kate mused.

She looked again. No, that wasn't it. Though there was an obvious close link, these weren't couples.

One of the women was tall and slim, and the others seemed to circle her and hang on to every word she said. She raised a bottle of beer to her lips, then looked round. Her dark glasses and baseball cap irritated Kate – so affected, she thought. Then suddenly as if she'd heard Kate, the woman took off her glasses and cap and ran her fingers through her short, dark, cropped hair.

Kate almost choked on her drink. Oh . . . my . . . God, it was her. Her daydream had come to life. Krista Starbright was here.

Krista seemed to notice Kate's reaction, and made some wisecrack to her friend. Kate heard them laugh and wasn't sure she appreciated being the source of their amusement. Embarrassed, she turned away and concentrated on watching the ice in her drink melt.

But, Kate couldn't help but look again. Krista was even more gorgeous in the flesh, tanned and well-toned. Even the small beauty spot above her lip looked different in this light. She wished she had the nerve to approach her, but instead she stared blindly at Krista, paralysed by fear. Perhaps Jan did know her better than she knew herself.

Kate's watch suddenly beeped, signifying it was time to go and meet Jan. Time to tell her it was finally over, that there would be no more ultimatums. She finished her drink and decided to visit the washroom before leaving. She gave Krista a final parting glance. Strangely, she felt elated but cheated.

The washroom was quiet as she opened the door and it wasn't until she was drying her hands that she heard someone enter. Momentarily she closed her eyes and wished.

Suddenly a woman's slender hands roughly cupped Kate's breasts from behind and started to unbutton her shirt. Cool air goosed her skin in contrast to the heat from the woman's hands. Kate's puckered nipples tightened further as the woman pinched them hard before freeing them from her bra. Kate moaned as the annoying, nagging ache between her legs intensified to knife-sharp pain.

Arrogantly the woman spun Kate round. Kate found herself staring into Krista's eyes. Krista responded by invading her mouth with a deep, thrusting kiss.

A noise outside made Kate pull back and she started to speak.

Krista silenced her by holding a finger to Kate's lips. "Don't worry," she said, "no one can get in here. Unless they make it past Ed."

Kate caught the glint in her eye and realized this woman was used to getting her own way.

Krista snaked her fingers down into the pool of waiting wetness and Kate's legs, firm until that moment, almost buckled at her touch. Tightening her grip, Krista pinned Kate ruthlessly against the wall. The surface felt cold and hard against her bare skin.

Then with a low, desperate moan, Krista pushed Kate's jeans lower. Helplessly wedged against the sink, Kate gasped as she felt Krista's hot poker-tipped tongue caress her.

She lifted her head and caught sight of her reflection in the mirror. Shocked, Kate almost didn't recognize her own image. Her long, blonde hair, always tidy, was hanging in total disarray. But the expression on her face astonished her most, flushed with sheer ecstasy and wanton desire.

Krista's tongue increased its rhythm in response to Kate's unspoken demands and knowing her release was imminent, Kate opened her legs farther.

But then all of a sudden Krista pulled away. Kate was bereft, angry. What was this shit? She wasn't some plaything to be used by someone who hadn't even the guts to come out. She saw an amused gleam in Krista's eye before tasting an unmistakable saltiness and feeling the fingers that were plunging deep inside her. Her explosion complete, she lay limp and totally spent across the sink.

Holding her gently, Krista allowed Kate a moment to compose herself.

"Consider that my autograph," Krista said with a chuckle, then kissed her softly before leaving.

Kate smiled resolutely. It was time to face Jan.

Fucking Rita for Julie

Leah Baroque

"Tell me again how you fucked her," Julie begs as she reaches up to pull the dildo strapped to my hips into the wetness of her cunt. She'd requested this story every night this week and no matter what I did with my fingers, my tongue, or our assortment of toys, she only came when I'd finished telling the story.

Two weeks ago, we'd decided to commit to a future of monogamous bliss. This should be our honeymoon; we should be lost in each other's eyes, yearning only for each other's touch. Yet here we are, unable to fuck without fantasizing about the waitress at the Italian restaurant down the road.

Rita was supposed to be my last one-night stand. My one last meaningless, no-strings-attached, nameless fuck. She was a piece on the side, but not behind my girlfriend's back. Julie had not only agreed to it, she'd instigated it. I'd been a bit of a party girl before I met her, going out most nights of the week and getting off with some hot new thing more often than not. And then I met Julie, at two in the morning at the laundromat round the corner from my house, both of us with broken washing machines on the same night. Maybe it was fate. Julie and I fell for each other, even though she knew about my past.

So at Julie's request, I fucked Rita. Being quite accomplished at one-night stands, I know that it's the few ground rules you keep that make it work: don't take them home, don't exchange numbers, don't speak of ever seeing each other again.

But Julie insisted I break my own rules – me, who had so few to begin with.

So that was how I came to be fucking Rita in the bed of my beloved, while she lay on the other side of the wall, listening.

That's what I thought this was really about: Julie's desire to fuck other people, vicariously as it were, through me. If it wasn't for the butt cleavage proudly on display above Rita's hipster jeans as she leaned over the table opposite ours to deliver a plate of steaming hot carbonara, I might have kept my head, kept some degree of control of the situation, and never let it pan out the way it did. But when I give myself permission, I'm very much the dyke version of all those hetero men controlled by the longing in their pants. A slave to the whims of the clit.

So there was Julie, on the other side of the wall, trying to be as quiet as she could be so that Rita wouldn't know she was there. The only noises I could detect were the squelching of the dildo entering Julie's cunt and the gentle clicking of her pink dolphin vibrator (when it's on pulsate it really sounds like a dolphin's playful song). To conceal the animal noises coming from the next room, I put Norah Jones on the stereo – at Julie's request. But if I was producing this epic, the soundtrack would have been Nine Inch Nails, something dirty and rough that you can really fuck hard to.

Julie bought me a different dildo to fuck Rita with so that she could use my strap-on. I appreciated the consideration of safe sex, but had to wonder if the real motivation was that she wanted to ensure that I would fuck Rita the same way I fucked her.

"Tell me again, please baby," she croons, looking up at me with sexual longing in those green/blue eyes that I can't say no to.

"We could hear you through the wall, fucking yourself, teasing your little clit with the dolphin," I say, drawing my nails lightly over her clit to bring her attention back there.

"Tell me what you did to Rita," Julie moans, pushing her cunt up towards me, inciting me to shove this pink dildo back into her to the hilt.

"To stop her from worrying about the animal noises I started moving my index finger in deliciously slow circles around her butthole."

Julie tries to turn over so that she can be on all fours, the way I'd fucked Rita. This was the only way she wanted me to fuck her lately. I'd let her have that but I wouldn't let her continue this fantasy. I spread her buttocks apart as I did to Rita, and play with her hot little butthole.

"And now I'm pushing this deep inside of you," I push the pink silicone deeply into her cunt.

"You're mixing up your pronouns. Talk about her not about me."

To stop her talking, I rub at her clit with my spare hand. There's no way she can concentrate on pronouns with this much stimulation. I push into her harder, pausing between the slow strokes to keep the dildo deeply inside of her with the base of it pressing against my clit.

"I'm fucking you Julie, only you," I whisper, linking my words back to her body by tracing my fingers around her clit. "Tell me you want me to fuck you, only you," I slow my actions down, threatening to stop everything if she doesn't vocalize what she wants.

"I want you to keep fucking me, I want you to play with my clit." She's close to coming and will agree to anything right now.

"Who do you want me to fuck?" I keep the circles around her clit slow and light, a promise of the sweet reward that is only moments away.

"Me, only me," she gasps as I insert my lubricated thumb into her arse. She whimpers with pleasure and pushes her glorious buttocks back against my probing thumb, the muscles in her back and buttocks tensing as she comes.

I grind my clit against the base of the dildo and reach my own climax just as Julie tells me we don't need Rita anymore.

Transit

Elfie Schumacher

She was taking it off. Knowing she was facing forward, I strained to see her; a light shone on her, and I could feel it on my lips. I found courage in a one-way view, soaking her in, minding her form. She took off her coat as the bus pulled away from the curb. I was three seats back on a slight diagonal, a perfect line drawn.

Some time had passed since this began, months even. It was my route, it was hers. Every day, every chance I got, I was dreaming the distance closing in. Without knowing so much as her name or the sound of her voice, I listened for the sound of her footsteps. I ate for a day on glimpses of her face. Wanting her created an intolerable tension, existential hell. I worked myself into this state through careful observation of her slightest movements, quiet worship of the nape of her neck, and painstakingly timing my morning departure.

But I was unable to do or say anything at all. Cursed with crippling, debilitating shyness, I let fear have it all every time. When she looked in my direction, I looked away. I dreaded, knowing that somehow I could never have her; breathing shallow, knowing she was on the same bus. Planning the day I didn't look away. I was tired. I didn't get much sleep the night before, and the last thing I needed was this mental loop.

Last stop, and everyone got off the bus. I had been so preoccupied with thoughts of her that I barely noticed. The bus driver had already gone for coffee. I finally started to get up when I felt two hands on my shoulders, pushing me back down. I turned to see who it was but a hand shoved my head against the window. Then I heard her voice whisper in my ear, "You think I don't know? You think I don't see you, eyeing me?" She laughed softly. She slowly turned my head around, our eyes meeting in the stark morning light. Her eyes were dark, steady, intense. She held the look for a second and then her lips were on mine. She kissed me deep, like she'd always known how to kiss me, lips full. That kiss shook every part of me. Then she let go suddenly and walked off the bus. The driver returned and said, "Let's go. Last stop."

A couple days went by, and I didn't see her. I felt some strange combination of elation and nausea. Each day that I approached the bus stop, my heart was in my ears, in my boots. When I thought about that kiss, I felt exposed, like every part of my body was naked. I had no plan, I had no recourse. Only one plan seemed possible; eyes to the ground. I had been caught stealing, and as a result feared I'd see a gleam in her eye. Worse yet I had no idea what she would do next.

On the third day since I'd seen her it was raining hard; and when it rains hard in Vancouver, bodies multiply on the bus. I stepped on, and started pushing my way through the throng, smelling like wet dog. Just as I reached the back of the bus, someone stood up to get off and I quickly took the seat. I noticed the familiar hands of the person next to me. Her hands. I'd sat right next to her. I just could not look at her face. I stared ahead. I became conscious of her leg against mine, just enough contact to create a pulse where our thighs met. We were on the Main Street bus from Hastings all the way to 65th, where it turns back. At 49th, she and I were still sitting at the back of the bus, and there were only two people left seated up front.

Suddenly I felt a sharp jab in my side. I winced, looking down to see what it was. A knife glistened just below my right rib. I was facing her now, and she wore a lop-sided grin. She leaned into my ear. "Unbutton your pants. Pull down your zipper." Her words were soft yet forceful. I hesitated, and the knife dug in a little. Silently I did as she said. I looked up – 52nd. Underwear still intact, she put a hand on my thigh, her head moving in closer; then slowly, deliberately, her lips drew circles over my clit. It was more than I could take, the fabric a thin veil. She drew wetness from me to the fabric molded to her lips. My hips gyrated, sweetness rushed to my head like a hallucinogen, my vision slightly blurred. All I could feel was my blood, the world reduced to a point between my legs. That's when she took two fingers, and pulled my underwear to one side. 55th. Her tongue slid over me, I felt a rush and bit into her shoulder. Every stroke sent sharp waves of pleasure to my core. She had momentum, faster, harder, until I shook and buckled over. Zip, button. 64th. 65th. The bus came to a stop; I bolted out, turned the corner, and sprinted.

The day at work was a blur. I tried not to think about it, but occasionally the mental image slipped past my guard and I blushed violently at my computer. By the time I was walking towards the bus stop to go home, I was wondering how the fuck I should interpret this. The woman who made me weak, who had seemed so untouchable, had just . . . I threw my head back and laughed loud and hard. Sure takes some nerve, I thought. Handsome as the day is long, and not a bit shy. Maybe even crazy. But in my case, you can't force the willing.

Dress Up

Andrea Miller

On the dance floor two women are grinding into each other. One is wearing jeans so tight the fabric clefts her lips; the other is wearing a short black skirt that tempts me toward darkness. Still thinking about their femme on femme appeal, I snap my head up and look around for Alex, my butch girlfriend.

I've only dated butches. I've never even touched a femme. I'd thought they were too much my mirror until Alex got out of the bath one night and changed my mind. Her hair dripping, her skin glistening, I watched as she wrapped herself in a towel. In the steamy flicker of candlelight, the terrycloth looked like a dress, strapless and tight to her breasts. And her mouth, bruised from my hard kisses, looked painted.

That was a month ago. Now I find myself watching women with low-slung jeans, lipstick, and lacquered nails. Now I want Alex to dress up for me. To let me see how it feels to slide my hand up her skirt. But Alex, all beer and swagger, won't play that game. "Not once," she says. "Not ever." And I say, "Alright, there are other games."

One game we both like, which we're playing now, is to arrive at the bar separately. I wear garters and no panties. She wears baggy jeans straining at the crotch – something extra underneath. Sometimes she finds me perched on a stool and I don't realize she's beside me, at least not until I feel her fingers climb my thigh to touch the lace where stocking meets skin. At other times I find her by the dance floor. I come up from behind, put my hands on her hips, then breathe into her ear, "Second stall from the left in ten minutes."

Always the first to get there, Alex sits in the stall, waiting to hear my heels click on the pink tiles and my soft knock. Inside, I unzip her fly and her cock, purple and large, springs into my hand. I bend down and give the head quick flicks of tongue, melting into longer licks. I swallow the shaft, feel it rub against the back of my throat. Then I slip a finger under the harness and into her pussy, slick and swollen. Above me Alex moans, then pulls me up and turns me towards the wall. I part my legs, cock my ass in the air, and wait for the thrust. But she teases me, just grazes my pussy with the tip until I'm panting and straining down on her dick. Only after I've thoroughly juiced my clit and thighs, her fingers and shaft, does she slide into me. Slowly at first – then faster – until the whole stall shakes and quivers with us.

That's what usually happens. Now, however, I can't find Alex anywhere. I scan the dance floor again for her red baseball cap. Then, giving up, I head for the bar. Halfway there we come face to face, but I almost don't recognize her – she isn't wearing her baseball cap. Instead she's wearing heels and a skin-tight white dress. Her tomboy hair has been gelled into a pixie cut and her lips glisten crimson.

My mouth is a circle of shock when Alex leans into my ear – "Second stall from the left in ten minutes." I reach for her arm, try to say something, but she's already disappearing into the crowd, the slits in her dress flashing leg.

Tonight I arrive first, still reeling with surprise. The lights are dim and, from here, the music is not much more than a pulse. I lock myself in and I think about her ass in that dress, two tight globes with a cocky wiggle. Then I think about her hand unfurling inside me, finger by finger, and my pussy starts to get wet.

When Alex finally knocks, I'm stroking my clit. I let her in and press my fingers to her lips. My taste makes her growl, makes her kiss me hard with teeth and tongue. Her kiss makes my cunt throb, makes my tongue writhe with hers. Her mouth still on mine, Alex lodges her thigh between my legs and we grind into each other. The thrust of her hipbone is sharp, almost painful, but I can feel her sex on me too. My hands find the slits in her dress and slip under the folds. I push her dress up over her hips; then kneel down on the cold floor. I pull her panties to her ankles and leave them there – wet, white, lace visible on both sides of the stall.

As I begin to drive my tongue into her, Alex moans and leans back against the wall, cool and smooth. I circle her clit and suck her lips – teasing her until she knots her fingers in my hair and presses me hard into her cunt. Then I trace her hood with my tongue, find her clit and lick her into a slow rhythm that gains force as I follow her thrusts. Soon her thighs start to tremble and she comes against my tongue: her hips rocking above me, her juices smearing my face.

► ► ►

Minutes later we walk by the femmes – still grinding on the dance floor. But this time I'm only thinking about Alex and the purple cock at home in the bottom drawer. Only thinking about how it will feel when she straps it on. Only thinking about how it will feel when she buries it to the hilt.

Impossible

Jannit Rabinovitch

I asked Jody to stay after work. She timidly stepped into the construction office, camped in the living room of the old house we were renovating. The site was quiet. Everyone else had left: the only sound, cars outside on the downtown streets. Jody stood just inside the doorway, nervously rubbing one hand up and down her muscled arm. A hint of sunlight made the hair on her arm glow golden and filled the room with the scent of toasted sawdust.

"Lee seems to have taken an instant dislike to you. You better watch yourself," I said.

She looked up startled, pushing her hair off her face with her sturdy fingers. I was the project co-ordinator. It wasn't what she had expected when I asked her to come to my office after work.

We'd only been on the renovation site a week, but already Lee, who was in charge of the construction crew, had made her feelings quite clear. She didn't like Jody, and didn't trust her. But I didn't trust Lee, even though I had been her supervisor on the Women's Construction Project for months now.

I convinced myself that I was talking to Jody because she didn't deserve to be harassed. She didn't. But that wasn't the only reason I wanted her to stay after the others had left. I suspected that one of the things Lee hated about Jody was precisely what drew me to her. She exuded sexual energy. I wanted to prolong our chat as long as possible. She was leaning against the door frame with her arms crossed, waiting for me to say more.

"How do you like the job so far?" I asked, searching for something to say. Her clothes, her hands, her nails were filthy from tearing apart walls filled with decades of dust and old insulation. I wanted to take her home and wash her strong, capable body. I wanted to run my hands over her lean stomach like she was doing now, absently scratching her midriff. My fingers began to tingle.

"It's okay." Then she volunteered out of nowhere, "Tomorrow's my birthday."

"Really? Let me take you to lunch." My words had a voice of their own. They seemed unaware that it was impossible. I was twenty years older than her. I had a girlfriend and so did she; they both worked on the project. I was the boss and she was one of the crew.

"Yeah, sure, Sandra. Sounds good," she said over her shoulder as she walked away. She held my eye with hers for a moment. "Tomorrow, then."

I sat down hard and forced myself to breath. What was I thinking? It wasn't too late. We could just have a polite lunch and nothing more. But already I wanted more.

Little Black Dress

Joy Parks

Mom always said every woman needs a little black dress. But it was you who proved how right she was.

You're on the phone with your back to me. You don't hear my heels on the carpet. You don't know what to do when you turn around.

The soft black velvet strains tight against my breasts, my waist. You're speechless. I stand in front of you, hands on my hips, my legs parted, my lips parted too and stained with color. I'm close enough for you to smell the French Vanilla oil warming on my skin. You stutter. Cough. Make circles in the air with your hand, willing the call to be over. You never take your eyes off me.

Finally, you hang up. You sigh. Your eyes are wide, a warm, soft blue. Lust does this to you. It's this that makes me want you so. What my femininity does to you, how it makes you younger, wilder, braver. I want the passion you believed you had forgotten, that butch boldness you thought long gone. I want to be the one who makes you feel exactly what you're feeling right now.

You move towards me, arms outstretched, grasp my shoulders with your hands. You kiss me. Touch your lips to my neck. Your hands slip lightly over my breasts, and my nipples firm instantly under your touch. Your breathing changes. You lean closer, whisper my name into my hair. I feel your lips at the base of my throat, your tongue grazes the neckline of the dress, then lower still, you taste between my breasts. Denied this so long, we're both still surprised at how brave desire makes you.

Your history overtakes you. Your stance shifts, your legs part, your body is tight against me now, forcing me against the wall. You arch your back, your pelvis forward, you begin to slowly grind against me. Your hands are everywhere. You're sighing louder, breathing my name. I want to will you under my dress, command your fingers inside me. But I won't. I want you to run the fuck.

I remember your excitement the first night I used that expression, how amazed you were that someone my age would know the passion those words would unleash in you. You came out the year I was born. Still, you tell me that I understand who you are so well, that I know what you need better than any woman ever has. It's instinctive, you say. And when you finally stopped fearing the years between us, you called it fate, a sign that I was meant to be yours. I remember too, how well you fucked me that night, whispering "mine, mine, mine" as I opened to take your fingers inside, how I wrapped my legs around your shoulders while you tasted me, took me, claimed me. How I knew that I would never belong to anyone the way I belong to you. That's what I'm doing now, letting you take me. Letting you run the fuck. Knowing what this does to you.

You part my legs in one simple motion; you've done this before, with more women than I need to know. You look at me, your face hard with desire. You kiss me. Then again. Then you smile. My skirt is pushed up; I can feel the cool of the wall against my bare thighs. I think about your stories, the ones you whisper to me in the dark, in bed, at night. Tales of you touching women in doorways, back alleys, dark city streets, too young and afraid of being caught to get a room. Left with no place to love. We have a queen-size bed upstairs. The couch is there in front of us. But no, right now, this is what we both need.

You slide your thigh farther between my legs, grip my hips, press hard against my wetness; you're letting my cunt know your strength. You're still proud of your thighs, their firmness a reminder of your athletic days, your swashbuckling times, when anything and any woman was possible. You love it when I ride your thigh, how my wetness makes your pale skin slick. You love the details of sex: the unexpected words desire forces from us, the scent in the room, the wet spots on the sheets. And you love to watch, cool as stone, as I lose myself in the pleasure. You're proud of what you can do to me. You've got that look now as you slip your fingers inside my panties, graze my wetness. You shudder, kiss me hard. Feel me open under your hand. You won't make me wait much longer.

I cry out when your fingers finally reach inside me, I crush against you, I want to spread my legs wider, bear down. But I wait, I let you take me higher, wait to hear you beg me to come for you. And I do. I would do anything for you, anything to make you feel this wanted. Yes my love, I will teeter on heels for you, let you fuck me up against a wall, be your slutty young femme in a tight black dress, I will take your fingers inside me and writhe, scream and drench your hand, rake your shoulders with my painted nails. There's no end to what I'd do to make you feel this way.

Later, we go for a drive. You swing your fifty-six-year-old woman's body into the driver's seat like a teenage boy. You hum love songs from the radio, touch my arm, kiss my hand while you drive, kiss my lips at red lights. You open my door, take my arm when we walk, your steps like a dance, you're strutting now, your body remembering how it was meant to move. You seem taller, louder, every bit the proud and swaggering butch you were born to be. And it's all because of my little black dress.

Jeanie

Tamai Kobayashi

Too many drinks in too many bars and she just wants one good fuck. Damn that Jeanie. She leans against the cold rail and that clears her mind. She can walk, anyway. Then in the elevator of her apartment building she spots him.

Young, but not too young, handsome but not a muscle man, leather jacket and torn jeans and a nice friendly smile.

She smiles back, realizes she's seen him before.

She stumbles and he catches her, holds her arm. A gentleman.

God, she wants to fuck him.

An invitation to her apartment. He's quiet, though. She kisses him and places his hand on her breast.

It's inside her door that she tells him. Not without a condom.

He steps back, rocks on his heels.

She finds a condom in the pocket of her purse, tugs on his leather jacket, leads him to the bed. She strips, fast, she wants this so bad.

He is quiet.

Shy, she thinks, and laughs at the thought of seducing him.

She spreads her legs. Fuck me.

He can see her, see how wet she is for him.

Turn around, he whispers, staring.

She turns, on her hands and knees, and feels his hands on her ass, his kisses, his tongue. His fingers part her slit and she rocks as he works his tongue deeper.

A gentleman.

Fuck me, she wails, but he takes his time.

She hears the tear of plastic wrap.

Don't turn around, he whispers.

But she feels it, the tip, skirting the outside of her cunt, and she pushes down to reach it, but he pulls away.

His hands grab her hips as she's wiggling her ass, eases it in slowly so she can feel every inch, a vicious jab at the end, pulling out.

She gasps. He's playing rough now.

In again. He feels so different, so hard. She tells herself it is the condom, this angle, she's never done it like this before.

He grunts, as he plows into her, so hard he lifts up her knees. Nothing gentle about it.

Faster now, his breath blowing, he hasn't taken off any of his clothes, but she's so naked, opening, thrust by thrust.

She likes this, wants it badly and she goads him with her cries.

He pulls her to the edge of the bed, thrusting wilder, so hard he's ramming her, she's coming, coming, crying out begging, fucks so fiercely she feels him plunging into the deepest part of her, ripping her apart but she's taking it, this movement, her cunt coming, she can't hold, crying, cursing, stomach lifted off the bed, spasms riding bucking hips slapped down, fucking cunt clenching she comes, like rolling thunder, electric spasms, twitching, holding him in.

She rests, panting. Sweat beading on her back.

He's still hard inside of her. Moves so slowly. Begins again.

She can't believe it, hasn't even begun to recover, but so easily aroused, her body responding, a low and snarling groan, hips tilted ever so slightly to take him, not that he's even sliding out, how easily he stokes her, nudges, coaxes the juices out, she can even hear her wetness, the sticky slurp of dick moving in and out, but he starts, short staccato thrusts as she begins her keening moans, takes her faster to the edge, growling if she can take it, he fucks her deeper, stabbing, moves his hips a different motion, so hard, still so hard, how could he still be so hard, she's coming, wants it faster, too much, too much, she'll feel him days later, pain skirting the edge of pleasure, she wants him to come inside her, feel him wither in her cunt, tries to hold out but she tumbles, muscles rippling, hands slapping the bed, fast, an orgasm so deep it's no longer a release but a sobbing fucked-out need.

He's still inside her. Hard.

He slides out. Sees the pussy lips, swollen. He's churned her, cunt bubbles, frothing.

She turns. See him, lying back. His dick. His rubber dick.

She rises, cunt aching, falls, slapping, arms flailing, falls against him, feels breasts, the binding through the denim shirt, the slightness of frame.

He turns her, pulls her off, pins her down, her grunts, spitting fury, but his mouth on her breasts, as he thrusts, grinding her into the floor.

He fucks her so mindless and rutting, this fuck-bursting, cunt-pumping joy, this movement as she opens and opens, jumble of sweat smell and wetjuice, this calling, the only god she's ever known.

▶ ▶ ▶

When she wakes, she sees her, examining her swollen cunt.

Jeanie, she scolds, that was a bit too much.

Jeanie leans forward, looks at the woman's pussy. Contrite, she asks, I didn't hurt you, did I? Jeanie licks her clit, as the other woman wriggles. Pushed away, Jeanie looks up but she can see her cunt is swimming. Jeanie knows she likes it hard.

The woman picks up the harness and straps it on. Smiles. She knows Jeanie's bluffs and blusters, her hungers, her rewards. She knows Jeanie at midnight, Jeanie in the morning. But there's something else she wants to know.

This time my fantasy. She rolls Jeanie over.

Your ass is mine.

The Homecoming

Elaina Martin

After weeks of silence, the beautiful woman I loved is knocking at my door, and I almost can't believe my eyes as I glimpse her through the peephole. I greet her with a huge smile and hug, hoping she can't see the whirl of emotion beneath my surface. I figure as long as I'm calm and poised on the outside, I may be safe.

After a few awkward moments, we settle into the conversation of what we've been doing since our last meeting. The talk is both serious and playful. I tease her, and she responds by flirting back. As the conversation progresses, it becomes clear that, despite being apart for a relatively short period of time, our lives have changed dramatically. This excites me, as I realize it does her. I want to prolong the visit, so I invite her to stay for lunch and set about boiling water for tea. She's always loved my cooking, and agrees without hesitation to share the stir-fry I've decided to prepare.

We continue our conversation as I chop the vegetables. I try to focus on what she's saying, but I'm so excited by her presence that I can barely concentrate. I finally ask the question that's been on my mind since she walked in.

"What made you decide to stop by?" I ask cautiously, trying to keep the bald desire out of my voice.

She hesitates and I turn my back to her, pretending to give all my attention to preparing our meal so she won't see my nervousness. When she begins to explain that she hasn't been able to stop thinking about me, her voice is suddenly so close, the distance between us erased. I turn to find that she has moved from her spot in the sitting room to stand directly behind me, practically leaning over me. I can feel the rush of adrenaline, blood and longing move through my body at warp speed. My eyes meet her gaze, and I consciously let go of all the control I've worked so hard to maintain. I want her now, and I give myself up to desire.

Lunch preparations are forgotten as I turn and pull her to me, enveloping her in my strong embrace, one hand clutching her hair, the other gripping her slender waist. Ravenously our mouths meet, tongues like two women dancing, probing one another. Without letting go, I begin to manoeuvre her towards my bedroom. She puts up no resistance as I scoop her into my arms and carry her the final few feet down the hall. Her tongue continues to circle my own. The elation of having her so near leaves wet through my jeans, and the ache between my thighs begins to build.

I know what she likes, and I throw her roughly down on the bed, holding her arms above her head. As I hike up her skirt, I run my fingers through the crevices of her hot, pulsing cunt, and then tear the blouse from her body. She offers me her body, and like a greedy, half-starved child I begin to feed on her, running my mouth over her lips, neck, breasts, stomach, and finally her ass. I find her cunt hot and open, her clit throbbing, her body heaving in the desire for me to take her. She moans and sucks at whatever part of my body she can reach while digging her hands into my flesh. I poke my tongue inside her beautiful cunt, and fuck her like that, taking all that she has to offer. With both arms, I spread her legs and lift them high so that my tongue can find the sweet spot buried within the folds of her.

I move one hand to join my tongue, thrusting into her deeply, driving my fingers home with the speed and strength I know she likes. I continue thrusting hard and fast, never losing contact with the slippery saltiness that signals her desire for me. I breathe in her scent, hungry for the taste and smell of this woman who reminds me that I am fully alive. With her head back, mouth open, she begins to come, calling my name in guttural gasps. My hand inside her is awash in her fluids as she comes to me. She moans with pleasure in the aftermath as I lay my head on her pubic bone. I revel in her beauty and sensuality. I'm her bitch, and she knows it.

As I move up to snuggle against her, I see by the look in her eye that she knows she has me once again. Not satisfied in her knowledge, she moves to take me with the same frenzied passion I've just let loose on her. She pulls at my clothes, biting my breasts. I am so wet I feel like I might drown us both. The fist that slips inside me feels like it never left and I am riding a wave of ecstasy and euphoria. Her strokes are hard and deep, exactly the way she knows I like it. I give myself up to her in complete submission to her will, and come in one long wail like a dam that's just burst.

As we settle contentedly into one another I think how I've missed her cunt, the way she tastes, the way that only *she* can take me. I seem to float above looking down at the remarkable sight of us tangled together. I know I am still in love with her.

In the moment that I begin to acknowledge and admit my love, the smoke alarm begins to shriek. The stir-fry is burning. Laughing and scrambling to reach the kitchen, I think how lucky it is that I've already eaten.

If This is It, I Want Out

Carolyn Norberg

A·SEX·U·AL

1. Having no evident sex or sex organs; sexless.
2. Relating to, produced by, or involving reproduction that occurs without the union of male and female gametes, as in binary fission or budding.
3. Lacking interest in or desire for sex.

► ► ►

The day after my first sexual encounter with a woman, I taped the meaning of the word "asexual" to the center of my bathroom mirror. I highlighted definition number three in red. An asexual was my new term for what I was going to become. Though it would take some practice.

The night before this realization, I had been at friend's party. After six too many tequila sunrises, when we were outside smoking the last joint, some woman decided to pull a strawberry-seduction routine on me. "I think I'm getting a vibe from you," she said, as she brought a fresh strawberry to her mouth and flicked her brown hair over her shoulders.

"You are?"

"Oh, most definitely. That three-year relationship you spoke of earlier, the one that recently ended – was that with a man or a woman?"

I wanted so badly to lie, but I told her the truth. "It was with a man," I said.

Her eyes went straight to the ground, and she turned and placed the strawberries down on the picnic table. I took a puff on the joint. She started talking to the people behind us. I stared at her back. I began wishing I had qualified my response to her with something more revealing, but I didn't know what. As soon as she started to walk back inside, I took a larger puff on the joint – I had never slept with a woman before, so I had to think quickly.

"I'm *bisexual,* though," I called out. The woman stopped, spun around, and grinned. She walked back towards me, picked up a strawberry, and gently brought it to my lips. I blushed as I chewed on the berry. "Spend the night at my place?" I asked. I couldn't believe the question had come from my mouth, nor could I believe the ease of her reply.

"I'd love to do that," she said. "Lead the way."

She took me by the hand and smiled. I threw the joint to the ground and she stepped on it. I don't know what I was expecting, really, but I remember thinking, at that precise moment, that being lesbian must be easy – it had never been that easy to pick up a man.

It was me who placed the last strawberry onto her tongue.

▸ ▸ ▸

We staggered along in the summer rain and climbed the stairs to my apartment. On the porch, my hands and tongue were all over her. Her lips were soft and tasted like tangerine lip-gloss. Her wet hair was dripping all over the floor. We instantly moved to the bedroom where I threw her onto the bed, so that I was standing and she was lying. I had no idea how to please a woman, but I was about to find out. I tore her wet black dress open and licked her hot, sweet-tasting skin. The room was starting to spin, but she smelled like fresh lilacs, so I had to keep going. I bit down hard on each one of her erect nipples, which made her moan. I was feeling born to please a woman.

But then I passed out.

▸ ▸ ▸

In the morning I woke up to discover that some woman I knew nothing of was sleeping next to me. I didn't even know her name. What would my grandmother think? When I sat up the room was spinning, and I felt an immediate need to puke. I ran to the bathroom and threw up violently. I splashed cold water onto my red face, then I stared vacantly at my reflection in the mirror. Who exactly was looking back?

I wanted that woman to go home immediately. I wanted her out of my bed. I stomped back into the bedroom to command her to leave, but the naked stranger was, now awake smiling at me as she stretched her arms seductively above her head, "Good morning, Sunshine," she said.

I opened my mouth to speak, but couldn't. She stood up and walked towards me. I tried not to look at her body. This time, *she* pushed *me* onto the bed.

"I'm Miranda," she said, standing over me. "In case you've forgotten." She pulled my T-shirt up and smiled at my erect nipples. "Bisexual, hey?" She looked at me, and I nodded my head. "I hate to tell you this," she said. "But bisexuality is usually where it begins."

When she bit on my right nipple, I moaned. I ran my fingers through her soft hair. *Tomorrow, yes tomorrow, I will work on becoming asexual.*

Good at Math

Donna Allegra

I could leave the party now and John couldn't fault me. From behind a slatted wooden trellis where ivy climbed I watched as, frosted glass in hand, he postured for three of his cronies – badly aging frat boys bent on picking up scatterbrained girls in skimpy dresses. A woman stood in their midst. She wore a red liquorice shirt-jacket atop pleated moleskin trousers.

Booze-bleary, John made a show of throwing his arms around her. She allowed his embrace with neither enthusiasm nor coldness, and listened cordially when he spoke, while the other men watched her closely. I'd describe her as having the face of a young god – her look strong and self-directed, not coy or seeking to appeal to anyone.

"And not married yet?" John asked.

"Never had an offer good enough to do me in," she said.

John's neck retracted like a cobra's. "What's so bad about being a wife and mother?"

"Why don't *you* take it on as a lifetime career?" she said.

"Aw, you'll get married. Single people are lonely," Bill said, his face pouchy and saddled with sadness.

"Never. I get too much company listening to married friends' troubles. They always tell me how lucky I am to be free," she laughed, cheeks flushing in a way even red blush couldn't impart.

John scoffed, his voice urging her to agree with him, the threat of disapproval darkening his timbre. Would she resist or refuse? Tone of voice was always his lure for herding people in.

John and his friends had circled her. Their pack formation wasn't only about her good looks, although her skin shone with a rise of honey and sunlight. I've often wondered how men can stand the beauty of women. But as I saw her body brace, I thought they can stand it the same way I do: savor the attraction and leave her alone.

"You're a tough career lady who's good with numbers, so do the math: the clock ticks on that nesting instinct. . . ." John said salaciously.

"Oh, I think —"

"Don't think," John interrupted. "You're not equipped for the job." He stamped his boot, amused with himself, as the other men laughed. She, however, just smiled politely.

"Oooh. Got you there, Makeda. But you know I'm just joking. Hell, I'm the man who brings people together," John said.

She remained composed, her teeth clenched, eyes on ice. "Don't look so glum, Makeda," John said. "This is a party. What will these future CEOs think if I can't throw my weight around with project managers?" he said, winking at his buddies.

She looked as vulnerable as an egg. I don't know I simply didn't leave and spare myself this kind of aggravation. But it was driving me crazy to see him jab at her and get away with it.

I had on a strappy black dress with side slits and enough cleavage to pass muster. I moved closer to the group and the men all paused.

John's eyes brightened through his not-drunk-just-numbed state. He made an elaborate show of taking me into his arms.

"Aubrey." John squeezed my waist, but I wanted to shove him through a glass door. "Tell my business associate here that I'm an equal opportunity offender. Besides, I'm a great matchmaker," he said, inspecting my boobs. "Nice . . . dress, hon."

"Johnny, we've had this discussion more than once." I pitched my voice to that of Indulgent Mommy. "It's not nice to offend people." Having scolded him, I allowed him to pull at me as if we were a couple. Now he wouldn't have to show the men that no woman bossed him around.

"Oh, Makeda doesn't mind. She's used to me by now," he said.

Makeda raised her chin and braced herself as if John were going to throw up on her kidskin pumps. But her stance softened with a willingness to let go of her barely-hidden anger when she looked my way. I felt keen attention from her.

"John, my man, more sustenance," Mike said, and Bill raised his glass. Tom followed, chanting, "Drink, drink, drink."

Seeing his real audience had lost interest in the game, John said, "You girls wait right here, I'll fix any hurt feelings in a jiffy." He shoved past us to follow his friends.

"Well, that was delightful," she said with exaggerated good cheer. "Makeda Ali." She extended her hand; I felt excitement tingling through my fingertips as we shook.

"I'm Aubrey. John was awful. You deserve a medal of honor for grace under fire," I said.

"John's a crass act. But he signs the vouchers that pay me," she sighed, taking a well-earned sip from her glass. "Black cherry spritzer," she explained. "You schmooze heavily and drink lightly if you're a girl who knows what's good for her career." I warmed to her combination of vulnerable and smart.

"And in business, friends are few and enemies abound so a woman must behave well, regardless of provocation," I said, which made her smile.

It was time for us to move apart, in the dance of polite conversation. But we stayed put, our eyes meeting then skittering away. We turned to hear the bar area detonate with laughter.

"Must be a Viagra or blow job joke. Men go crazy over that," she said. But I also sensed her interest in me that was more than our shared loathing of John's behavior. Maybe I was getting good at this woman-to-woman thing. But how do you woo a woman, and not just wish after her?

"I want to ask the same rude question John put to me," she said, her face in the geometry of a question. I braced myself to answer.

"Are you married?"

"My divorce is in the final stage. Part of our agreement involves my – keeping up appearances," I said, careful to not name him.

"John," she breathed with dawning awareness. Good at math.

"And," I said, perhaps over-eager, touching her arm, "you and I should get together and do something. Or nothing," I said.

Makeda was still puzzling over the combination of John and me. It wasn't a simple equation. Her frown made me hesitate.

But my nerves melted when she said, "Yes, John does have a reputation for bringing people together."

(F)E-Mail Trick

Vaughan Chapman

I got an e-mail from this woman I met on the mountain last Sunday. She'd wanted my address so badly at the time, she wouldn't let me go until I gave it to her. And hey, I'm not saying I didn't want to give it to her. I mean, I was glad enough when she asked that I took my time searching my jacket and blue jeans for pen and paper. I thought I found something in my breast pocket, but it was just some leftover from before I decided to get in shape, a Tootsie Roll wrapper that I pulled out and rolled between my thumb and forefinger, shooting her a glance as I did. I was breathing hard.

I hunted through my day pack too, where I found two or three Swiss army knives and a pen, but no paper. Not even in my wallet. Only my license, ten bucks, a quarter, and an emergency number in case they found me at the bottom of a cliff and needed someone to come and pick up the pieces.

Last time I listen to my friends about taking a bare essentials wallet with me when I go hiking.

This woman couldn't find any paper either, and I swear she was blushing as she searched her breast pockets and down the front of her pants. I'm not saying I didn't get a little warmer. Might have been the hiking, though.

Without a shred of paper between us, I said I'd give her my e-mail address if she'd give me her hand.

It was like being in the movies, if you know what I mean. Not *at* the movies, but *in* them. In one. Ours. She looked at me with eyes that glinted like the gold I've been chasing my whole life. All I wanted was to reach out and brush my hand through her short, auburn hair and bring her head close enough that I could see myself in those bright eyes, in some nice house on a couple of acres with her Suzuki Sidekick and my Nissan X-Terra in the driveway, and a couple of popcorn-white bichons sitting on the verandah in the sun.

I waited. She grinned. The dimple in her left cheek winked at me. I waited some more. She took off her glove. I held my breath. She waited. I held my breath some more. And then and there, at 1,500 feet, she gave me her hand. Time stood still. As if a movie camera were zooming in slow motion until the entire shot was just her bare hand.

Half a dozen chickadees flitted in the poplars beside us. No babbling brook, though. No plane overhead flying banners. No theme song that everybody'd be humming. Not even anybody else on the trail. Just her hand – and mine making for it with that pen that looked kind of symbolic, if you know what I mean.

I wrote my e-mail address on the palm of her hand, no fumbling, no losing my nerve. But her hand was so hot from the hiking that I offered to blow on it so her thighs, I mean the ink, wouldn't smudge before she got back to her car. She lifted herself. I closed my eyes, put my lips up real close, parted them. I could feel the heat of her, almost taste her. She groaned. Or maybe I groaned, I don't know. I was feeling pretty weak in the knees by then. It was my first time.

Hiking since I decided to get in shape, I mean.

Like I said, I got an e-mail from this woman I met on the mountain last Sunday.

A Letter to Aunt Peg

Lyn Davis

April 15, 2003

Dear Aunt Peg,

Remember when I used to spend the summers at your house, and you'd come into the living room to do your sit-ups and leg lifts? You'd never do them when Uncle Denny was home, but you didn't care if your daughter, Carol, and I were around.

You'd go into your bedroom and close the door and change your clothes. You'd come out into the living room in your robe, then pull the robe off and lay down on the edge of the couch. You'd have on shorts and a bra, and you'd tuck your feet under the edge of the couch and begin to lift your shoulders and back off the floor, into the air, then back down again. The part of your breasts that were tucked into your bra would never move, but the part above your bra would slide forward, then back, with each sit-up. Forward, then back. Forward, then back. After about 100 sit-ups, you'd turn around and lay with your hands under the couch. I could see the couch move as you adjusted your grip, but I couldn't see you. Just your legs lifting into the air, then back down. Up, then back down. Fifty times. Your calves were rounded, muscular, and your thighs were dense, the muscles gliding up and down under your taut skin.

You'd finish, heave a big sigh, and then slip your robe back on. You'd pop your glasses back onto your sweaty face, your robe still undone, because you were "hot," you said. Then you'd go into the kitchen with us girls to supervise as we made dinner since we were only eleven. You'd get close to us, ask us what we were doing. I'd see beads of sweat on your collarbones, your cheeks, and sweat pooled around your neck before rolling down that beautiful crevice and into the mysteries held tight by your white cotton bra.

Every time you came into that kitchen, I wanted to ask you to sit down, let me sit on your lap. Every time, I wanted more than anything to bury my face into that fold your breasts made between your bra and your neck. To inhale the sweet scent of your sweat. To roll my face to the left, then right, and burrow deeper; roll left, right, again, burrow farther down. I wanted to place my hands beneath the cups of your bra, feel for myself how heavy your breasts were, find out if they were as firm as the rest of your body. I'd feel at home, safe there, I knew.

And I felt something else. Something I didn't feel again until the next summer when I held your daughter in her bed, kissed her face and neck. I wanted to kiss her skinny flat chest where we both knew her breasts would some day be, but she said we were just practicing. I knew I wasn't – this was the real thing for me. But I was afraid that if I disagreed, she wouldn't let me do it, and I wanted to. I wanted to badly enough to lie.

I still think about your face, the compactness of your short voluptuous body, and those summers. Where I used to feel guilt, I now feel only desire.

Thank you for those summers, Aunt Peg, and for creating the space that made it safe for me to begin to find my own true self.

Love always,

Lyn

Oceans, Lakes, and Ice Cream

Judy Lightwater

Meeting her the first time felt perfect, like a quiet path through the woods, trees tangling with each other and crossing their branches so beautifully. She had grey in her hair and a job she liked, something to do with kids. I spent two weeks thinking about her jacket and her jaw line before I called.

"I'd love to," she said to canoeing and a swim, my standard first date in good weather. I have few dates in any season, but best to think of something I would do on my own if she canceled. In keeping with this policy, I had an ocean-side picnic with a luscious woman last summer. But we had absolutely nothing to say. Tuna sandwiches and the view of Mount Baker kept us occupied for an hour, then it was time to go home. Next Sunday, I'll get in a boat with this new person and see what happens. Kissing? Getting close enough to smell her? But that's paddling ahead of myself.

Sunday arrives with a slight breeze and blue sky all around. "A little higher," I suggest as we hoist my battered boat onto my old Toyota.

"I haven't been paddling in ages," she says. "Everyone has kayaks and I'm not into that yet. Do you get out to the lake a lot?"

"Once a week in the summer, if I can. Makes me forget I'm in the city."

"My parents had a lake cottage when I was a kid. We spent every summer there. Lakes smell so different from oceans." Her hair is short and stops at her neck quite beautifully.

"I went to camp every summer to escape my family," I say. "The dock smelled like sun and Coppertone." We laugh about the days when sun tans were our primary goal, along with shaving ours legs and getting to the boys' camp across the lake for dances on Saturday nights.

Soon we're paddling towards my favorite rock. She ties us up easily, not afraid to handle a rope or climb the rocks a bit – important traits in a lover. I strip off my clothes and let the sun hit me. She glances at me but stays dressed. We occupy separate towels, our water bottles and snacks lined up on the moss between us. "I'm going in," I announce, and am soon stroking across the lagoon. No other swimmers or boaters here, we're too far from the main beach.

Finally, I see her shed her clothes and walk down to the water. Medium-sized breasts, a bit of a belly – delicious-looking, all told. As she slides into the lake, I don't say anything, just check her out subtly as I swim.

"Perfect, isn't it?" she says as she starts a steady breaststroke.

"The longer I'm in, the warmer I get," I blather, wishing instantly for more sophistication. She carries on, bound for the other side. I head back to our rock and haul myself out, collapsing on my towel in the sun. Modesty is hardly my middle name, so I feel no need to assure her I'm not trying to hawk my wares. When she returns, her T-shirt goes on quickly. I gladly observe her legs.

We're quiet for a few minutes when she asks, "What do you do when you're not canoeing?"

"Work as an editor, write, talk to myself. The usual stuff," I say. "How about you?" The scent of the lake water is still on us.

"School, these days. Can't believe I waited until I was forty-five to go to university. And decide to be a lesbian." I heard that about her, but it sets me back. I, too, was heterosexual once, though it's hard to remember now, like a book I've read but no longer recall the plot of, or why I thought it was important.

The rest of our time goes well. No kissing, but lots to talk about as we lounge on the moss of the giant rock. When we paddle back to the main beach, I feel so relaxed I don't care about being witty. We stop for hot fudge sundaes, and she touches my arm to make a point as we stand against the car. I move a little closer. The parking lot heats up and we make plans for a movie next week. When I drop her off at home, we hug goodbye, and I smell summer on her neck.

The Long, Dry Spell

Sara Graefe

It's been so long, I'd all but given up hope. I'd been wandering the prover-bial desert for what seemed like ever, that I began to wonder if I'd forgotten what it was like to drink, to feel my insides turn to liquid.

"Don't look for her; she's looking for you," the psychic told me. She was a willowy earth mother with long grey hair, her reading a thirtieth birthday present from my closest friends who were worried I wasn't get-ting enough. Getting *any* was more accurate. The psychic clutched my hands, her green eyes boring deep into mine. We were sitting across the small Formica table in her East Vancouver apartment, blinds drawn. Our knees were brushing under the table, and I became aware of myself tin-gling, deep inside – the intimacy of the session was almost as unsettling as her message. She was much too old for me, and straight to boot, but I was so thirsty I could've leaned over the table and kissed her.

Instead, I heard myself blurt out, "What do you mean, looking for me? Where is she? When's she going to come into my life?"

The psychic just shook her head. "Just be patient," she said, releasing my hands and gathering up her weathered tarot cards.

The truth is, I felt that I'd already waited too long. My break-up with Amy had rattled me to my very core. I'd closed inwards, told my friends I needed space. Enveloped myself in a protective skin and waited for the old wounds to heal. As the years passed, I'd convinced myself that I was better off alone. But who was I fooling? Deep in the night, alone in the double bed, I would lie awake with longing, my body aching for someone else's touch.

Eventually I emerged from my cocoon. Attempted to pick up some girls, go on a few dates. Nothing seemed to take. I was worried that I gave off some kind of smell – stale flesh, the stench of milk long after its best-before date. "Maybe you're looking too hard," my friends kept telling me.

Don't look for her, she's looking for you.

"But how will I know her when I see her?" I asked.

"All these questions," the psychic said. "Just be patient."

She'll know when she sees you, because she's the one who's looking.

Yeah right, said my inner skeptic, as my chest muscles tightened to protect my withered heart. And yet part of me held out a faint thread of hope. I kept casting glances over my shoulder to see if she was looking yet, then realized that was probably cheating.

By the time she came, I'd all but given up hope. I almost missed her staring across the crowded room at me. A boy-girl with short blonde hair, jeans hanging low off the hips of her angular body. She smiled at me with this lopsided grin when I looked her way, her blue eyes sparkling with life. When my friend introduced us, her hand lingered in mine just a second too long. I was worried that if she came too close, she'd notice my parched lips, smell my desperation, and recoil like all the others. But no, she just stayed there, chatting, the rest of the party fading away as I developed tunnel vision – just her before me, glowing as she spoke, electrons dancing in the air around us as we made idle small talk. As the party dwindled, she pressed my hand and said she hoped she'd see me around, before disappearing into the night.

My friends were incredulous – no kiss, no nothing? I could've at least asked for her number. "But if she's the one, isn't she supposed to call me?" I pointed out.

My friends shook their heads, wishing they'd never taken me to that psychic – I'd just let a live one get away. But I knew this time I had to let go, let it be, and wait for her call.

And call me she did. We went for coffee, then ended up back at her place. The first time she touched me, just a brush against my arm, I thought I was going to cry, it had been so long. Instead, I started to burn. Her hand cupped my breast as her lips met mine, and suddenly I was on fire, my entire body waking up after a long sleep. Without a word, she lifted my shirt and found my nipple with her mouth, a sudden jolt as my clit snapped to attention below. She just stayed on my nipple, gently sucking, as I became wetter by the minute. *Yes, it was still possible.* My breast kept tingling as she came up for air. Don't stop, I wanted to tell her, but already she'd moved down and was fumbling with my belt.

Giving me a sly smile, she slid down my jeans, my Joe Boxers, then fell to her knees. Burying her face in my crotch, she parted my lips and tasted my wetness. I sighed audibly as her tongue reached my clit, and next thing I knew, I was spouting like a geyser. I cringed with embarrassment, feeling like one of those teenaged boys who gets off in two seconds – then remembered I'm woman, and let myself revel in the pleasure of orgasm after orgasm as she kept drinking me, turning my parched body to liquid, her moans meeting mine as I kept coming and coming. She was the one, alright, breathing life back into my being, resuscitating me after that long walk in the desert. I shuddered one last time, and she planted a final, delicate kiss on my throbbing clit. She rose gently, pulling me into a close embrace and that's when my tears started to come, tears of release and relief.

"I'm sorry," I started to say. "It's just been so long –"

"Ssh," she said stroking my hair. "It doesn't matter."

Doesn't it?

I met her gaze through bleary eyes and eased into a smile, even as the tears kept streaming down my cheeks. She was definitely worth the wait.

Rose, Milk, Mildew, and Dust

Shannon Kizzia

These blankets smell of grandmothers: rose, milk, mildew, and dust. A painting of Christ hangs above the twin bed; it was done on a slice of tree, glossy now, his patient face unchangeable as I shift on top of her, fitting my leg between hers. I grunt quietly against her neck.

In the cool of morning, the women left. The other women. The funeral was yesterday. We came home in the afternoon, post-graveside, post-open casket service where I couldn't stop being astonished by the fact that my grandfather just wasn't breathing anymore. She was still. It seemed the most unnatural thing in the world.

We came home and unloaded the refrigerator onto the kitchen table after having wiped it down with a cool, wet cloth. Seven women, strangely silent. Cold cuts, raw vegetables, Velveeta and pepper jack, summer sausage, sour cream, salad dressing, fruit, four Dr Peppers, and three RCs. We brought out things from the cupboards: crackers and bread, cakes, cookies, peanut butter. We feasted quietly, filling ourselves up. We were drained. My grandmother, mother, aunt, my two cousins . . . me and Tina. I looked at her across the table as we all ate in silence. My emptiness could not be filled with food. She looked straight into me. Knowing.

The others left this morning to go to the grocery store. Piggly Wiggly. A ten-minute drive into town. We stayed behind. Nothing was said as we listened to the screen door bang shut and Tilda bark, my Mee Maw's voice, "Hush now. Them girls sleepin'."

No words as I lay in my bed and Tina in hers. No sound other than their car starting and pulling out of the carport. The increasingly distant sound of gravel crunching under tires. And then the faint, small whoosh of Tina's covers being thrown back off her body. Then nothing. I pictured her, not daring to turn my head, warm, large breasts sloping braless under her white T with the leopard painted across the front. The thought of the round of her tummy beneath my lips, so inviting. Her pussy all warm and moist when my fingers part the way of her. My bed felt like a void, my body too thin and hard with the clench of tension; I hold my pain between the winged bones of my scapulae, the clutch of my stomach.

"Honey . . . ," her soft voice entreated and it squeezed two tears from each of my eyes. I rolled out of my bed, feeling Beethoven-heavy, prodigal. I honed in to her. I couldn't look in her eyes as I crawled in under the blankets, but when I came to rest in the crutch of her thighs, I knew her as my salvation and I wept into her chest.

Now I wet the curve of her neck with my tongue. She helps me strip my underwear down my legs. Her fingers find me guilty-wet and she sighs. I open my mouth on her throat and breathe as she strokes between my labia without hurry. I want to move on her hand. She lets me. I don't have the strength to hold myself off of her, so I rest my body on hers. I move my hips. She crooks her fingers. She whispers up to the ceiling, "It's okay," then turns her head toward me, her lips into my hair. "It's okay." I'm crying again.

I start to work hard against her hand and she lays her other one on my back. "Don't," she says quietly. I obey her with a sob. "Good," she whispers and tickles at my clit some more. She does it lazily, like sorghum molasses, and I give up, moaning against her skin.

It starts to rain outside. I can't come. I just want to orgasm, to blow apart, to be done with it. But she doesn't let me. She rubs her fingers across me until I surrender any last hope of this being about sex. She strokes me, slowing as she feels me now too exhausted to cry. Then she pulls her hand from between my legs and wraps her arm around my waist.

"I want. . . ." My voice breaks and I try again. "I want to put my underwear on," I tell her.

She nods okay and is patient as I work them back up my legs. Then she pulls me into her softness; I lay my face against her breast and I stare at the wall. She holds me until we hear the gravel crunch again. She releases me when I strain away, fearful. I stand at the side of the bed, shoulders rounding forward, ashamed.

"Look at me," she says, and I do. It's not expectation I see there. It's not a question, not a need, not instruction or anticipation. Only acceptance. That's all she is. I blink, bewildered by it, and then the screen door opens.

I want to say thank you. Want her to enfold me into her again so that I can feel safe. I say nothing, and I know she forgives me, but I feel so sorry anyway. And then the moment is broken as their voices filter through. And I flit my eyes away.

Grieving With You

L.M. McArthur

The heavy rains pound down onto the concrete parking lot as we pull in. You turn down the sun visor and check your makeup one last time in the mirror before going inside. You try to smile and I reach out to give your hand one last squeeze before we open the car doors. The clouds that loom over our heads are low. It feels like I can almost reach up and touch them. Even this early in the morning there is darkness like night falling.

Falling like the rain, falling like your tears. I remember the way we had cocooned ourselves on the couch watching our favorite television heroine duel the evil villain when we heard the phone ring. How your face and eyes changed as you spoke on the phone, your gentle, soft face. The face I caress each morning to wake you. Now I see the pain in your blue eyes as we walk up to the door. I look at you once more before we enter and you read my thoughts and nod your head. The door is heavy as I tug the handle to open it, knowing once we cross over there will be no turning back.

The corridor is absent of light. Inside, you hug people I only vaguely remember from family dinners. I reach in my pocket and hand you another tissue as the tears start to flow. I stand awkwardly, not knowing what to do, except what I want to do is hold you, caress you till the pain of the loss has gone away, even though I can't. Not in front of these people, who would rather I disappear from you, would rather I not be the constant reminder of who you are: a woman who loves women.

We sit down in our seats. Your grief saddens my heart. I place my arm around your shoulders, I don't care who sees anymore. You lean your head against me as the tears stream down. We stay like this until it is time to stand and pray, our fingers intertwined. Finally we stand for the last time and watch as the pallbearers carry the casket out to where he will finally be put to rest.

I breathe a heavy sigh and push the hair out of your eyes. As the service ends, you gaze at me with loving eyes that lock me in place. A thin line of mascara runs down your cheek. I whisper, "It never seems to work when you want." I wipe your cheek to show the evidence, you smile and chuckle for the first time in days. When it's time to go, you hold your hand out to me, and I take it as I have done a thousand times before. We amble down the aisle for all to see. I reach for another tissue as we continue our way to the reception where your family is waiting for us.

Ellie's Blue

Ritz Chow

"Hours before she died, there was a certain color to the room – a brightness or glare that held us," Ellie recalled as she pressed her hips into the familiar contoured edge of the pine table, cluttered with brushes and paper. "She said she had to go, then the nurse walked in." Ellie shook her head like a cat whose jaws clenched something dead that it wanted alive – to taste again the writhing instinct of survival. Her right hand scraped graphite over a curl of paper.

From across the small cramped studio strewn with rolls of canvas, bottles of pigments, and taped paper studies of shapes and shadows, Siu Lin rested her head on the couch. Sunlight streamed through the tall, steel-framed windows and warmed her upturned face. The afternoon glow illuminated areas on the ceiling where the paint had chipped off exposed pipes, and reflected twirling particles of dust. In Ellie's studio, marveled Siu Lin, even the air wove a vibrant texture, spun its own mad swirl of life. She looked up at Ellie's hunched figure: her T-shirt was torn at the collar and slipped off her right shoulder, revealing a slim collarbone and a freckled shoulder. Her serious work shirt with acrylic streaks of old inspiration.

Abruptly, Ellie put her pencil down, gazed at Siu Lin, then shrugged. "You know, I couldn't even decide whether I loved her or not. Whether she loved me."

"Maybe it's the kind of love you can't define."

"If you can't define it, maybe it's not love. But I'm sure there's a color for it. Just as love makes us red."

In the sunlight, Ellie blinked with fatigue. Her body was unaccustomed to stillness, wavering with kinetic indecision, whether to continue or stop. It had been days, maybe months. Her mother's dying seemed to have gone on forever; and then, abruptly, death. The ending seemed thin, strung out, watered-down, washed of substance and emotion. A thick hollowness recycled footsteps, coughs, and weak moans through her mind; it seemed that whatever had gone didn't wholly depart, as if in its reluctance some effluence remained. Sudden yet expected. Ellie was stretched taut with nights and hours of waiting and, now that the wait was over, her muscles had yet to recover, lay stiff with a constant watchfulness.

Siu Lin saw this, wanted to hold Ellie, but had sat down to watch, to listen. She was unsure of touch, of contact, of whether her arms would comfort or be a consequence of refraction. If she dared to push through the meniscus of Ellie's surface, would the light bend her arms like thin branches dipping from air into water? Who inhabited the rarer medium? "Hey, Ellie," Siu Lin said softly, motioning her over, "c'mon, come here for a sec. I want to read you my new poem."

To Ellie, colors had always emanated energy and texture; her body would align to paintings, would refigure itself with slick pink licks and tangerine whorls. With her lemon yellow tank top and shock of auburn hair, Siu Lin radiated an aura of childhood summers – a pool of sunshine on orange shag carpet, a curve of fiery amber between gingham curtains after a midday nap. Ellie sat down on the velvet couch, rested her head on Siu Lin's warm bare shoulder, and closed her eyes.

Against her closed lids, she sensed a thin veil of redness – perhaps her own blood tinting her blocked vision. Siu Lin's shoulder lifted as she read, her voice resounding a sure cadence against the distant blare of car horns, the squeal of tires, and the clanking radiator. Ellie's head floated on Siu Lin's undulating breaths and pauses. It didn't matter what the words were, and it did. Nothing and everything mattered: irreproducible colors, the texture of light in the room the day her mother died, her inexplicable need to recreate irretrievable moments, what past interactions demanded of her. Each minute, a life passes us by. It matters simply that we matter. Ellie opened her eyes, saw the rhythmic flow of Siu Lin's breasts as she enunciated her words: something about skin refracting light, that blood only glows red when oxygen illuminates it, that deep inside our hearts our blood runs blue. Inside out, we bleed blue, to that moment, to that second of that shade.

Ellie smoothed the fabric over Siu Lin's breasts, slowly but in exacting circles until nipples edged the cotton surface, pushed into her fingers as Siu Lin's breathing overrode her reading. Words fell as Siu Lin's arms lifted and the yellow knit of thread dispersed to supple sighs. "Deep inside," Ellie whispered, "I am blue."

Siu Lin reached down and in to find Ellie in her blue depths, in her exhausted weeks of waiting, in her gasp for colors to let loose upon her skin. "I . . . know," Siu Lin said, tonguing each syllable against Ellie's opening blue, then kissed her deep in her somber purple and serious magenta, kissed her wet to the other side of grief.

The Persimmon

Nina D.

She was my third female lover. Dark and dangerous, as addictive as the French cigarettes that smoldered between her petite fingers, she taught me the fine art of eating persimmons.

"Lay here where the sun is," she said, beckoning to me, passing her hand over the rich red of the satin sheet where it draped down the length of the chaise lounge, molten folds falling to the floor.

I tucked myself in the bed next to her as she balanced a crystal plate on her lap. Sunlight caught the facets in the etched glass, sending prisms leaping about the single red fruit placed at its centre.

"Do you know this fruit?" She gazed up at me from under dusky lashes. I shook my head. "No?" She laughed, her throaty resonance sending desire through my body. "Well, this will be ever the more sweeter, won't it?"

She laid the persimmon in the palm of my hand, the weight of it warm yet ethereal, its scent rich and exotic.

"Yes?" She smiled back at me from the depth of her dark orbs. "You can feel its smooth glossiness, can't you? The gentle give that speaks of untold softness just below the skin? I can see you do. Look how its contours hug your palm."

She plucked the persimmon back from my hand and laid it on the sun-warmed plate. "Here comes the best part." She reached across to the bedside table and retrieved a short paring knife with a slim black handle and slender gleaming blade.

"A persimmon yields only to a very sharp knife and a precise amount of pressure," she said. With an expert cut from top to bottom, she deftly sliced the fruit open. Two glistening halves of tender flesh lay slightly shuddering on the plate.

Her liquid dark eyes shot me a knowing look. "The rapture of eating this fruit is yours."

She slid the tip of her thumb between skin and flesh. A tear-shaped droplet of honey-colored juice ran down the length of the fruit, met the soft mound of her thumb and continued down the inside of her arm. Instinctively, I reached to catch it mid-flight with my tongue. She laughed. A second later, the heady scent of this cherished fruit ambushed my senses: spicy, sweet, warm, musky. The scent of desire.

"It feels almost sacrilegious to eat it, doesn't it?" she said. "I knew you would understand this. Its beauty is humbling, and makes you crave it."

Her thumb continued down the inside of the skin, the pink red flesh resisting only slightly, falling gently into her hand. And there it quivered, fragrant and beckoning, a tendril of pulp still delicately attached to its skin.

She reached out, the cobalt blue vein pulsing under the white of her wrist, her small palm cupped to offer me the fruit.

The first touch of tongue to fruit and I swooned. I was overcome with the need to greedily suck it into my mouth.

"Slow down. Do you want it gone quickly?" she taunted me. "Go ahead, ravish it, see if you are satisfied. I dare you."

I stopped. My throat constricted, tears caught behind my eyes at the thought of crushing this delicacy in my haste and hunger. I moved my tongue tentatively forward and tickled the tip of the fruit, then I gently slid it into my mouth, the tender flesh wobbling over my tongue, the flavor overpowering me. This, I realized, was heaven.

She set aside the plate, the knife sticky with the nectar of the spent fruit. Stretching back across the crimson expanse of sheet, her white shirt fell open to expose the delicate lines of ribs under pale skin where they met the concavity of stomach, she smiled at me. "Darling," she sighed, "after the persimmon, there is nothing else."

Pomegranate

Degan Beley

It was hot, like Hades. Hot, at least, like it never gets in Vancouver. Celia and I took a slow walk to the store; she had wanted ice cream, but we came back with cigarettes and two bags of fruit. The corner store on our street is never what you bargain for and for some reason they had huge, ripe pomegranates on sale for ninety-nine cents. We bought six, despite neither of us having a particular taste for them, and stumbled back to our basement apartment to sweat. I grabbed two Coronas from the fridge and flopped on the floor, but instead of joining me, Celia was picking through the pomegranates. It was a far cry from ice cream, I thought, but I left her to her treat. I cracked a beer while she cracked open the fruit's husk and picked at the glistening seeds inside.

I could feel even the few sips of beer going to my head. Motes of sunshine danced in front of me. My eyelids fluttered, trying to choose between wakefulness and sleep and staying stubbornly in limbo between the two. Then my eyes opened to watch Celia absentmindedly freeing another pomegranate seed, but it fell from her fingers and got stuck to her bottom lip. Her tongue arched out of her mouth like a tentacle, retrieved its catch, and carried it back to her mouth. Her throat moved silently as she swallowed it and I followed the journey of the next seed with my eyes: fingertips, lips, tongue, throat. The entire act was a seduction. I was fully awake now. I forgot my beer and propped myself up on my elbows to watch.

Another seed, then more were separated from their husk, split from their woody centre and lost into her mouth. Each movement seemed slow and deliberate. Calculated, almost. It was agonizing. She was savoring each seed individually, letting them burst in her mouth then allowing the juice to run down her chin and over her hands, stopping every few moments to lick her fingers. I was mesmerized. She must have known what kind of an effect this was having on me, but if she did, it wasn't apparent. She was focused on slowly, systematically eating her fruit.

There has been some talk in recent years that the evil fruit of Eve's undoing was not an apple, but a pomegranate. The facts make sense—pomegranates are native to the same part of the world as bible stories and they are generally known to go further back in history. Facts aside, the pomegranate is a far more exotically sensual fruit. There's really no contest: if you are going to use a piece of fruit to lead a woman to temptation, then it must be the pomegranate. I sided with Eve. She didn't have a chance.

Celia slurped back some juice and giggled. Temptress. I was driven to distraction.

I wanted to reach out and lick the sweat from her neck, throw the pomegranate on the floor, and devour her. The seam of my cut-offs throbbed like a secret and the thought of it was so palatable that I felt my leg move involuntarily towards her. But it would never do to interrupt her performance with that kind of vulgarity. So I sat still, and waited.

By now she was covered with red juice. Her lips and tongue were red and spots of it flecked the table in front of her. Celia grabbed a tea towel from the counter to wipe a spot of juice that had leapt onto her arm. There was a spot on her chin as well, glistening red, mocking me, but that one stayed. I pictured myself licking it off. A small thrill ran up my spine. She ate another one. I imagined licking it off starting at her ankle. This was becoming unbearable. Surely she would be finished soon. How many seeds could there be? In my panic I imagined an unending supply, tens of thousands crammed into the spongy husk, jostling for space, refilling endlessly as she ate them. I crossed my legs and felt the sweat slide over them. My underwear squelched. She reached up to wipe her chin and I thought I could see her laugh just a little into the tea towel. She was clearly enjoying herself.

Vixen. I would have her for this.

Her sweaty white tanktop clung to her and I could see the outline of her body, alternately soft and hard, body and bone. Beads of sweat rose on her arms like diamonds and ran off in rivulets. The spot of juice was gone, dissolved in salt. She wasn't wearing a bra and her nipples poked out hard through her shirt, creating harsh lines and shadows across the softness of her chest. Her lips and chin and fingers were now stained red and she had to stop occasionally to wipe them on the towel. I imagined them being sticky from fucking and the last traces of both pomegranate juice and restraint faded as she licked and sucked at her fingers.

I think I may have groaned out loud. Celia glanced at me, then turned her attention back to the pomegranate, moving even more slowly now, on purpose. I was doomed. A seed fell to the floor; even from the shadows I could see how fiery red it was, like an ember spat out from the fireplace. It caught the light of the sun through the window and held it, burning. I knew the feeling.

Then I looked up and found her looking at me, her eyebrow raised cockily, sparkling with mischief. She plucked a final seed out of the leathery husk and sucked it hard from her fingers, then moved closer to me to hold it to my lips. It glinted like a ruby in the sunlight and as I bit into it, my mouth filled with sweetness. I could taste seduction in it. It was better than I could have imagined.

"Do you like it?" she asked.

I nodded enthusiastically. I had discovered a new appreciation for pomegranates.

Fruits of Our Labor

Wendy Atkin

I miss Jacquie most in the kitchen. We conjured so many meals together, dancing around the tight space with a grace that could never be choreographed. The worn hardwood floors of that kitchen saw the most action when guests were coming for dinner and our bodies moved back and forth, switching places like scissors slicing thin air, occasionally bumping gently into each other near the sink, where the water caught the setting sun reflecting off our damp faces. Hers and mine.

It was just last summer when we made our own tomato sauce. The production line was wet and messy, spilled seeds all over the counter. Plunging my white hands into a pot full of warm seedy pulp, I felt the back of my neck grow hot. Lifting a mass of the red mashed fruit and stuffing it into the yawning opening of the tomato press caused an immediate sucking action. Pressing harder, I felt the tunnel contract and pull the wet mass deeper into its dark cavity. Red juice spilled over into a deepening pail as the fruits of our labor grew before our eyes.

We fell in love, naturally, in the spring, along with all the other buds weighing heavy on their branches. The long heat of the season that year yielded more strawberry flowers than my garden had ever seen, and by June the tiny stems were laden with heavy red fruits begging to be plucked. We crouched hip to hip in the earth and filled a white bowl. I set it on the dining room table and with a mischievous grin Jacquie filled her right hand with ripe berries as she passed by on her way to start supper. I pulled my sweaty shirt over my head and collapsed on the sofa, my body damp and flushed with heat as I dozed. I awoke to find shadows cast over the room and my body naked but for Jacquie's silhouette, everything obscured but the flash of heat in her eyes. She traced the outline of my entire body with a single perfect strawberry, its tiny seeds rubbing up against all the sensitive spots. The red juices began to bleed a little down my legs as she braced herself to come on top of me, crushing the last of the berry between our lips as my tongue slipped deep into her mouth, sucking strawberry juice and Jacquie all at once. We were both hot then.

▸ ▸ ▸

This morning Jacquie knocks before entering my house and pauses in the doorway to remove her boots. I feel numb at this cold new way we have with each other. I don't offer her food or drink, only a seat at my old oak table. She reaches for an orange from the bowl in its centre, her eyes never leaving mine, her lips never asking permission. Her fingers clamp around it, but not so hard as to squish its natural perfection. She puts the fruit to her teeth and tears off a morsel, then begins to pull off its skin, stacking the pieces of rind on the table.

I'm very quiet so as to savor the barely audible sounds of her softly pulling the orange apart. With her thumbs, she probes the centre where the sections cleave together, plunging deep to tear it open. The orange yields easily to her strength and she rips away two sections at once, glancing up at me as she opens her mouth to receive its sweetness. A tiny pearl of juice escapes the corner. I watch it suspended there, desiring to scoop it up with my finger and taste the drop on my tongue. Instead, Jacquie uses her tongue to lick it up into her mouth. I love watching her eat fruit. At this moment I crave to be citrus, imagining that if sweet juice rather than blood ran through my veins, she might pluck me, too.

Instead I sit here watching Jacquie as she finishes the last morsel of orange. But I know that it's not over. Just as I am wondering whether she will sweep that little mound of discarded peel into the palm of her sticky hand, she selects a fragment from the pile and holds it up to the sun streaming through the bay window beside my table. Then, winking at me a little because she knows that I know what is coming, she holds it between her teeth, gently scraping the pith onto her tongue. I tried this once at Jacquie's persuasion and my tastebuds proved too delicate for its tartness. She held the peel in front of my lips patiently, although I pursed them tight.

"It's the richest part of the fruit," she had said.

I shook my head vigorously.

"Come on, open up," she persisted.

Finally, I parted my lips for Jacquie, allowing the peel between my teeth and pulling a little of the pith into my mouth.

"Again," she persisted, and in spite of my repulsion, I yielded to her once more. Twice seem to suffice.

Today, I watch Jacquie scrape the peel bare until it shines wet, spent from relinquishing all its nourishment to her. My breath catches a little, wondering if she will offer a piece to me. Our eyes meet, too quickly, and I can sense with a sad heart that it is over. I feel helpless to move as she sweeps the peels off the table, pushes her chair back with a sudden scrape of the floor, and walks towards the kitchen to discard them. I place my fingers on the table, considering whether I should rise, too. I'm only a little surprised that my hands adhere damply to the wood. She turns to me once more and the sun catches her face. I know how Jacquie despises this kind of exposure and catch myself before uttering the words poised on the tip of my tongue.

"I have to get back to her," she says, as if spitting out the words, and then she strides across the room. As she grasps the cold brass round of the door handle, she turns to me once more, saying only this, "I wish it didn't have to be this way."

I sit as if glued to my chair, Jacquie's words sinking like bitter pith into the soft tastebuds at the back of my mouth as I prepare to swallow them whole.

What Might Have Been

Gabriel McCormack

The moon falls behind the bridge while we stand on the path by the water. I hold her hand in mine. My motorcycle leans against the small concrete wall and I feel a surge of contentment and excitement.

"I know after all we've been through that I have no right to want you as much as I do," I say.

She drops my hand and throws back her head. I wait for her to respond. She turns back towards the water and says, "Sometimes it doesn't matter how much you want someone. You can't control everything." She turns toward me and puts her hand against my cheek.

I look into her eyes and see the place I want to be forever.

"Things happen for a reason," she says. "You betrayed me so that it would be impossible for us to be together. That's our fate."

I look down at the pavement. I know she is right. We'll never be able to get past it. Betrayal is the one thing she can never stand. Ironically, I wouldn't have wanted it any other way.

I don't regret what's happened because I don't believe in regret, but the pain is still real.

I look into her eyes again and imagine holding her close to me, stroking her head as she buries it into my chest. I think of us jumping on my bike and riding back to my place. She'd hold on tightly, arms around my chest. I'd feel the air on my face and be pulled gently into her. She'd move her hands over my breast on the outside of my leather jacket and I'd smile, feeling her intentions.

I'd reach one hand behind me and stroke her leg, straining to reach her thigh, but not quite able to. I'd drive faster, needing her, needing to be inside her.

We'd arrive at my place and park the bike. Before we get inside we'd kiss gently at first, then more deeply and intensely. We'd stumble into my building, our lips still locked on one another. Once inside my apartment, I'd push her against the closed door and kiss her hard on the mouth, frantically pulling her clothes off, moaning, "I want you so much. . . ."

She'd muffle a response, then I'd pull down her pants and slide my hand along the inside of her thigh, rubbing up and down, grazing her pussy. She'd be so wet and I'd smile as I teased her with my fingers. I'd rub her until she begged me to go inside, gasping in my ear. I'd laugh and tease her some more.

She'd unbuckle my pants and try to touch me as I touched her. My breathing would increase and I'd want her more than ever. Finally, I'd push my fingers inside her, reaching up, feeling the warm wetness. She'd moan and say my name over and over and kiss me on the ear. She'd enter me roughly and thrust in and out as I did the same to her. She'd move out of me and rub my clit as I penetrated her.

Her mouth on my ear, I'd hear her moaning amplified in my body. I'd kiss her, thrusting as I licked and sucked her tongue. She'd come loudly and grab my hand to stop. I'd focus on her hand rubbing my clit, moaning louder and louder as I fell further into myself.

Finally, I'd crumple into her arms. I'd look up and see her with a smile on her face, stroking my head.

► ► ►

Instead, I stand silently on the path by the water, looking into her eyes. I sense she knows what I am thinking and that she is thinking it too.

"I'm sorry," is all I can say, and I am.

I jump on my bike and ride away.

Gutter Girl

Sybil Plank

She was the woman everyone wanted: the hard-faced, strong-jawed, sweet-mouthed woman. You know what will happen and you know what she is when you see her sitting in the hazy light like magic sliding across her pouting mouth and sculpted chin. You know when she looks at you with her half-sneer, you'd lean forward and kiss her if you had the chance.

You had shaped the gutter girl into what you had always wanted, this girl of your dreams, the phantom girl who rocked and drank and reeled her way through life. She's always drunk and she'll go to a terrible death, you always said. But oh how you loved the drama of it all.

The gutter girl dreamed of slitting herself open and watching her blood flow, like thin honey, like thick water, like grey in a black and white movie. If you turn out the lights, blood loses its color.

The gutter girl told a story about Mom and Pop and the trailer park life of dirty dishes in the sink, the scrabble life of playing in a yard made out of gravel. Home was a rusting trailer perched among others hot in the sun, like glare on the steel rails, full of people poor enough to dream of wooden windowsills and a patch of green behind a house.

You loved all the stories the gutter girl told you about the hard life. You said it gets you off and almost makes you want to come. At first you thought the girl made it up for fun, but the girl wasn't laughing as she talked about thirst that all-night whiskey drinking cannot ease. When she was a child, she played hide in the shadows behind burnt-out cars and the wreck from the last family who had suddenly packed up in the middle of the night. Their trailer was left behind to nest with the birds and mice, their yard filled with used condoms and an old mattress sodden with rain.

The gutter girl told you about lying on the ground and watching the stars while she hid. She did not say what happened when she was found.

The gutter girl knew how to slap just right, how to leave a pale mark like a red bruise fading into blush. The gutter girl wiped her eyes with the back of her hand and pretended it was sweat and you never noticed as she said, "I'll tell you what you want to hear."

In the morning the gutter girl said she didn't remember your hand all the way in as she opened up and asked for more and wanted the clips pulled tight. She came with the sound of your voice against her throat, but she wasn't really there and in the morning she forgot everything.

She told another story about a pebbled stream slicked shallow behind the trailers and how the poplars smelled sweet and dry as their leaves clattered in the monotone of heat.

The gutter girl whispered that she didn't mean forever, and you wanted to lie on the floor and curl up and cry out, bawl out sorrow, and shriek for wanting her to stay, even as she walked away.

You try to remember that what she said will make a good story. She is already a character you fucked, as if she were the real thing, as you took it all in and opened up for more. In the story, she always comes back and slides her hands over your shoulders and down to your breasts as you wait for the pain that's like a sharp knife. It would be better than hearing her laugh and watching her stand up and walk out the door.

Sometimes the gutter girl wakes up to a cool morning and a sleeping woman, and then is gone and vacant like the thin flame of a candle that's so easy to snuff out. The gutter girl knows what it's like to disappear. She knows what it takes to turn her back on a sure thing as she walks away into another day, where she can be someone else. Just look at her and ask for another story.

Not Here

Mary Davies

Friday night.

I am in my dead sister's friend's truck. It's raining, and we're talking about poker, which Patricia loves and I know nothing about.

"I always wish I knew, it looks so cool," I say. I drink more of the beer she brought, start to feel my head loosening. I love this feeling. It makes it easier to kiss her like I used to want to do.

"I'll teach you," she says. She veers off the Rotary, up the hill onto the 103. I don't ask where we're going.

It's weird to be with Patricia like this. When we were nine and twelve, she doubled me on her bike, taught me to skip rocks when my sister wasn't there. Now I'm eighteen and she's twenty-one and I don't even have words for what we're doing. Mom and Dad will be worried, but I can't stand the weight anymore of being the sister who didn't die. It's been two years.

I don't want to think about then. I just want there to be a now that lasts and lasts. I suck the rest of the beer from my can.

"Want another one?" Patricia asks.

"Sure," I say. She reaches for the bag on the floor in front of my feet, swerves onto the gravel shoulder, quickly pulls back onto the highway with both hands on the wheel.

"Whoa!" I say. "I'll get it."

"Sorry about that." She laughs, stomps on the gas. There are no other cars on the highway.

I just laugh, crack open the beer, have a big cold swallow.

She pulls onto the gravel shoulder again when I say I have to pee. The wipers swish furiously.

"Here?" I say, still laughing. "I'm gonna get soaked."

"So?" she says. She's not laughing anymore. I can't tell what she's doing.

"All right, I guess I'll just get soaked." I open the door to climb out. I stumble into the ditch next to the road. A car whizzes past, red tail lights in the dark. I pull down my pants, pee on the grass. My hair's soaked and my sandals are squishy.

I'm trying to pull up my jeans when I hear the truck door slam, look up to see Patricia block out each headlight as she comes around the front of the truck, hops down into the ditch. She's sucking on a beer. She throws the can behind her, then puts both arms around me, pulls me to the ground.

"Wait, I'm trying to get my pants—" I start to say.

She pushes me into the weeds. A stone's pressing into my back. Her mouth's warm and wet. My head feels dented from the bumps on the ground. Suddenly her hand's between my legs, rubbing.

"What if someone drives by?" I say.

She doesn't answer. I hate it when she stops talking. She keeps kissing me and rubbing. She makes a sound like, "Mmm."

I let her. I don't fight. After all, I try to think, it's supposed to be romantic, making out, or whatever you'd call this, in a field. In a rainstorm. Only it hurts and it itches and I'm starting to get cold. She keeps kissing and rubbing. I don't know how to make her stop. I won't come, I'm just numb there.

She kisses me again. My head grinds on pebbles. Finally she gets off me, tries to help me with my pants. "Wait, I've got rocks in my ass!" I say. I burst out laughing again, trying to brush them off. I tug the soaked denim over my damp skin, finally get my jeans zipped.

In the truck, I start shivering. I grab the last beer. She puts the defroster on high. She is focused on the road. I suck hard on the beer. "Where are we going, anyway?" I say, squinting through the windshield.

▶ ▶ ▶

I try to avoid her morning tongue when we wake up at her aunt's in Petite Riviere, say I have to pee.

"Mind if I jump in the shower?" I call from the bathroom. My head is splitting, my belly feels seasick, but I am wide awake.

"Go ahead," Patricia calls. "Towels are in the linen closet in the hall."

The shower's strong and hot. It's almost eleven, but feels like early in the morning. We were still awake when it started to get grey at the window, even in this rain. I stand under the water a long time. I wonder how I lost my excitement, my thrill of her first kiss, her touch, the secretness of us, and why now I just I feel annoyed and smothered by her.

The shower water starts to cool. I soap up, rinse, start to shiver before I'm done. The towel's thin and rough. I dry off, wrap up my hair, pull on last night's clothes, which stick to me in the steam. I put some of her aunt's Crest on my finger, rub around my teeth, gag and spit. Stand in front of the foggy mirror trying not to feel so tired and too grown up.

I am not the sister who died. I will graduate from high school in twelve days. I have a job and some free studio time in my painting teacher's studio in the evenings to keep me from home. And I'm sleeping with another girl. I sigh from the weight of it, feel like a girl in a book in a long tired story.

I hear Patricia walking around the kitchen. "Want eggs?" she calls, banging a pan.

"Sure," I call back. I run her aunt's comb through my hair. I can't stop shivering. The rain beats on the window. I open the bathroom door. My sister's not here. It hits me like a kick in my gut.

Friends and Lovers

J.L. Belrose

People have become my windows; my vision is more and more through their eyes and voices. Of course, I'd reclaim my full 20/40 eyesight if I could; that goes without saying. But I can't. And that's where all the tumbling circles converge. I can't change what's happened. For five months I've been adjusting. Accepting what is. Making jokes so people around me are more comfortable. Telling myself, and convincing others, that life will go on the same – almost the same – as always. When a lover leaves a dark curly hair embedded in the soap, you don't see it. But you survive.

I can't find her nipple. I see her shoulder, the contour of her collarbone. I move my hand toward it, wanting to trace the ridge with my fingertip, but the target and my hand disappear.

I have peripheral vision. I'm not blind. My central vision dissolved in less time than it took the traffic light to change at Carlton and Jarvis. Stopped on a red, I closed my eyes for a moment, yawned, looked back at the light and it wasn't there. Nothing I focused on was there. Only edges. A horn blasted behind me. I reasoned the light must be green and I somehow got through the intersection and over to the curb. I put my head back against the headrest and shut my eyes, convinced that I'd open them again and the world would be normal. But it wasn't.

I fumbled with the cell phone. "Helen, I've got this weird fuckin' headache. Can you come get me?"

"A migraine?"

"I guess so. It doesn't hurt, but my eyes are funny."

"It's a migraine," Helen said, the way she states what she decides are incontestable facts. "Where are you?"

It turned out to be macular degeneration, of which approximately ten percent of cases are the "wet" kind in which vision loss may be rapid and severe. Of course, if there's ten percent of anything, that's where I'll be.

► ► ►

Arms and breasts and legs have different textures, different temperatures, different degrees of firmness. Her breasts are softer than her belly, and warmer, almost powdery, to the touch. I find the nipple. The nub defined now, although the areola's still smooth, not puckering yet. I hear her laugh. This one vibrates in the throat, expectant.

► ► ►

Helen loves me. I know that. She's kind and, in her own way, she's patient. It's funny; I didn't see this in her before. Or maybe she's changed. Of course, she's still cranky sometimes. And I wouldn't have it any other way. I'd rather take a scolding once in a while than have her be sweet on me all the time like some friends, well-meaning but too patronizing, are inclined to do.

There was a time I doubted Helen's love for me. Around four years ago, after we'd been together three years, she brought up the subject of an open relationship. "If one of us happened to meet someone we were attracted to, wouldn't it be better to be honest about it?" she asked. "And work it out so our relationship made room for it, rather than let it divide us?" I replied with tears, accusing her of wanting to leave me, then finally said, "Just don't tell me about it, okay? If you're going to do it, just do it, and don't tell me about it." "That's totally not the point," she said, then stomped away.

It's funny that it was me who was the first to test the idea. I'd met Anne at a women's health conference. It started with coffee and girl talk – centered mostly, I admit, on my insecurity and complaints about Helen – and progressed to a couch in Anne's small, plant-filled apartment. It ended in another coffee shop when I realized Anne was making plans for a future with me that excluded Helen. But I'd never stopped loving Helen. In fact, despite my bitching, I loved her more than ever.

► ► ►

Her pubic hair is soft and tangly. I let my fingers run through the clinging curls. I used to think it was coarse, a nuisance that had to be swept aside, but now it acts like a welcome mat to my hand, inviting me to enjoy and linger. "Oh God, what's with you?" she says. "You're turning into such a tease." Her voice is all puckish and earthy.

I drop my head to where I think her breast will be and nuzzle into the soft flesh, then open my mouth and use my lips and tongue to navigate the globe, seeking the island that is her nipple. She tries to speak, but if there are other words, they're swallowed, sucked into the force that lifts her against my hand. My fingertips collide with slippery heat and slide magically into her opening. We've always connected easily. Nothing has changed that.

"It can work," she'd said. "An extended family. A network of friends and lovers." Tempered by my experience with Anne, I'd agreed. And . . . it's worked.

► ► ►

Helen is still in the shower when I hear Valerie's key in the door. Val comes into the kitchen where I am, clutches me from behind, and nips at my neck. "Be careful," I say. "I think I've maybe spilled juice on the floor."

"I'll get the mop," she answers, then instructs me to stay off the living room carpet until my slippers are cleaned. But first, she barges into the bathroom where Helen is toweling herself. I hear the grunting laughter and muffled noise that is their horseplay.

When Helen is dressed, ready to leave for work, she comes to me. She hugs me and whispers, "I love you."

I say, "Call me later, if you get a chance," knowing she will and that we will survive. I will survive. We're a family. We're all in this together.

Lavender Shoes

Miljenka Zadravec

Sean's dead.

Vanessa's gone. Working on the Rez in Ontario.

Jude just got married.

Here I am.

Clean and sober and all alone.

Except for my memories.

I don't want the story to end like this.

I dial up Vanessa. During the day. Can't wait for the cheaper evening rates. She and I plunge deep into conversation without any preamble. My voice is shaking as I tell her about Jude.

"I overheard them talking in the café. I hid my head in my book and listened. Deb was giving the details of Jude's wedding. Wedding! I thought I was going to throw up. She said Jude was getting married in a church. I couldn't believe it."

I am crying. Swallowing hard so I can keep telling Vanessa the story. "I wish I didn't feel this. But since I heard about Jude I just keep crying and crying. . . ."

Vanessa's voice is soft. "I totally understand, Marica. In some really sad way I'm glad Sean killed herself. Otherwise, I'd still be caught up in that insanity, whirling around like a feather in a vortex, not able to let her go."

I am shocked by what she says, yet I desperately need her to understand.

I stare out the window at the dark clouds about to unleash a torrent of rain on the city.

"I don't want to be with Jude. Six years of that rollercoaster ride and I had to get out. But I feel so much rage that she's going to live 'happily ever after' while I'm still dealing with feelings about her." I am gripping the phone hard.

Vanessa's voice jars me. "Marica, don't think that for one minute anything has changed. Jude is still living that hellish life. Do you think she's stopped drugging and drinking? Do you really think because you finally walked out on her, that any of that insane, game playing, obsessive jealousy and rage has stopped?"

I listen to Vanessa's voice rise and fall with her emotions. I know she is thinking about her relationship with Sean: her inability to leave despite the drugs, the chaos, the fighting. Remembering that Sean finally left her.

It's been four years since I left Jude. Yet today I can only remember the life we shared: Jude singing to me, being silly and romantic; her crooked grin charming me, her green eyes staring into mine over mugs of cappuccino at Nick's Cafe. We were so merged, there was no boundary between us. She consumed me. "Vanessa, I can't stand these feelings. I know I walked out on her. I left . . . but she was the only woman I've ever been passionately in love with. No one else."

Vanessa's anger shakes me out of my reverie. "Jesus Christ, Marica! It's amazing how quickly we forget how awful it really was. How badly she treated you."

I stare out my window. I am picturing Vanessa at her art table, paints and brushes around her, her long, dark hair and high cheek bones framing those deep chestnut eyes. She is Jewish, but her features would easily blend with the Native kids she works with.

"I know, Vanessa, she was cruel and moody, but I can't stop thinking about what I heard in the café. That they were getting married in white tuxedos and lavender shoes. I hate it." I spit out my words, knowing that I hated what Jude and her partner proclaimed to share. Intimacy? Commitment? The same pair of shoes?

Vanessa's voice is soft now. "Sweetie, it's okay to cry, even if it makes sense to nobody but you."

"Fucking lavender shoes! Jude was always such a hopeless romantic." I can feel my throat swell up again. "I feel like I'm in a bad lesbian soap opera." I joke trying to lighten the mood.

Vanessa doesn't laugh. Her voice is full of conviction. "Marica, maybe you need to shut the door on Jude. Let someone love you, someone who treats you well and doesn't make cocaine the primary lover in the relationship." Vanessa's words are sharp. They bite with truth.

Perhaps memory is a liar. And good friends, more reliable witnesses.

Perhaps.

Vanessa and I say goodbye and as I hang up the phone, images of Sean flash in my mind.

Sean: hanging with a rope around her neck in the bedroom she shared with Vanessa.

Sean: passionate, Metis, covered in tattoos and track marks.

Sean: whom Vanessa adored and tried to leave over and over again.

My memories are deeply embedded. Sean, Vanessa, Jude: with me forever like some kind of crazy glue.

I imagine Jude standing at the altar, with her white tuxedo, her silly crooked grin and her lavender shoes. Would she be stoned? Oh, probably.

So I do the only thing I can. I walk across the street to the drugstore, buy a glittery wedding card and write on it, "I wish you peace."

Back outside, I stand at the top of a hill. I look west and see the clouds are beginning to separate: huge radiant beams of white light shimmer against the dark clouds. I saunter down the hill towards Commercial Drive, walk into Nick's Café and order a cappuccino. I raise my cup to Jude. For old time's sake.

Rock Bottom

Giovanna Capone

I'm in the back kitchen of Jorge's Uptown Enchilada Bar watching Gloria chop tomatoes and dice cheese at lightning speed. She holds up a small cube of Monterey Jack. *"Quieres?"*

"Gracias," I say, popping it into my mouth. She continues dicing. When I first started visiting her here, the older women in the kitchen thought I was Mexican. They would talk to me, rolling off a stream of Spanish r's and words I didn't understand, except they sounded like Italian, only faster. Now I *comprendo* a little Spanish, from having lived in Texas for three years.

They call me *"la Italianita,"* saying *"Ella esta en la cucina,"* pointing me to Gloria. They know me as her friend from New York.

"I ran into Nicki the other day," Gloria says, passing me another cube of cheese.

"Where?" My nerves get jittery just hearing the sound of her name.

"In the Safeway."

"The booze aisle?" I say, picturing my girlfriend cruising the Jack Daniels. "I'm not speaking to her these days. She's too wild."

"Pobrecita. You need a home girl."

"She's anything but that. Nice woman. It's too bad. We have so much fun together when she's sober. She's a great dancer. We like the same bands. We have a ball, as long as she's not drinking."

"Drag her to AA," Gloria says, scooping up handfuls of cheese.

"She'll never go. I wish she would. I love her. But I can't do it anymore." I consider Nicki's troubled childhood and wonder if I'm being completely fair to her. I remember the stories of her father's abuse, her mother's silence, and how she ran away at the age of fourteen. Guilt starts to set in. Am I giving up too soon?

"Well you've only known her a few months, haven't you?"

"Four."

"Girl, that's no time at all!"

I glance around, wondering who can hear me. "I mean, I finally meet somebody I like, and now this? Why's it so fucking hard to be with the woman I love?"

"*Chica*, maybe you should circulate. Meet somebody new. Hey, you're one of the most eligible dykes in town," she says, throwing the last bits of cheese into a bowl. She bends down to grab some onions from a sack under the counter, then disappears into the walk-in freezer.

I smile, thinking I'm one of the most eligible dykes in town. For about thirty seconds I snap out of my usual despair over Nicki, and feel good.

Then I remember how Gloria met Cindy. One day she told me about Cindy's past. She grew up dirt poor in East Texas, and was a crackhead for years before they ever met. When they first got together, Gloria realized Cindy was addicted. She made her get clean, insisted on it. Took Cindy two long years to dry out. Gloria hit the roof when she first heard her lover's story.

Cindy had been tangled up in some drug and prostitution ring that operated out of Sally's Place, the women's bar downtown. The owner was behind the whole scheme. They pulled in young lesbians who already had a habit by supplying them with easy drugs in exchange for prostitution. Cindy's habit was full blown by then, and she was being set up with different men every other night.

Gloria said, "I should kill those scumbags."

She picked up her .38 one night and almost went down there herself. She was going to clean that shit up single-handed. She knew that the sleazebag who counted the money at night was a major kingpin. The only thing that stopped her was Cindy promising she would get clean.

"Shit!" Gloria punched her fist into the palm of her hand when she first told me the story. "I woulda killed that ringleader. But I didn't wanna end up another spic in jail." So she made Cindy keep her promise. She nursed her through a two-week withdrawal, and the girl kept her word. "She's been clean ever since," Gloria told me, with pride. Helluva story, I thought, and remembering it, I felt renewed hope for Nicki and me.

Not long after Cindy dried out, something else happened. The prostitution ring was exposed. Two of the biggest drug dealers were busted. News spread like wildfire and women began boycotting Sally's Place. This all happened before I came to town. The bar was shut down for good. Now there's a better club, Chances, a mixed bar, with both gay men and lesbians.

Gloria drapes a dish towel over her shoulder. She's a hero to me. She lays a small bowl of guacamole and chips on the counter. *"Quieres?"* she says. "You gotta keep your strength up. You got places to go, things to see, people to do." She picks up her knife and starts slicing onions, her brown arms moving quickly over the chopping board.

The next day, I'm wiping up ketchup and smashed French fries at Burger King. We were told this morning they'll be installing time clocks in a month. All the Burger Kings in Texas are changing to a time clock system. It's bad enough around here; now they'll be watching our every move.

Two more hours before I finish up. I carry a load of plastic trays to the back room and dump them in a sink of soapy water. Somebody taps me. "You got a phone call."

I pick up the receiver in the back room and it's Nicki. "Why are you calling me here?" I whisper. "I can't talk."

"I fugging can't . . . do it . . . anymore . . . I fugging . . . shit."

"What's going on?" She sounds drunk. I barely understand a word she's saying. My heart starts pounding. "Shit, Nicki! What happened?"

She tries to speak again, but her words are so slurred, I can't understand her. I whisper into the phone. "Do you need a doctor?" She doesn't answer. "I'm coming over there," I say, slamming down the phone.

I wipe pickle slices off the last dish tray, wondering if I should call 9-1-1 right now. Shit, Nicki, why do you do this? I've talked with her before about getting a counselor and getting sober. I glance at the clock, dump some half-eaten French fries into the trash, and sneak out early.

When I get to Nicki's house, the curtains are drawn. She's passed out on her bed, still wearing a white T-shirt, cut-off jeans, and the studded leather bracelet I gave her. I smell alcohol. Her blonde hair is dyed bright green, half-spiked. I sit down on the edge of the bed. I love this woman, but I hate seeing her in this shape.

"Nicki, what happened?" I shake her, but she doesn't answer. I pull her upright and call her name again till she finally groans.

"Nicki, you gotta stop this. Can't you stop it? I love you." I pull her close to my heart, flashing on that talk this morning with Gloria. I decide to say everything that's been on my mind.

"Nicki, I want a life with you. But look what you're doing to yourself. You're ruining our chances. I want a real life with you, honey. Not this," I say, as the tears start rolling down my face.

"Sooo tired," she slurs, and falls back on the bed, her eyes half open.

"Nicki, this is too weird. I hate seeing you like this. You could've died." I scoop her up again and hold her against me. Minutes pass as I think about Gloria, and what she went through with Cindy. But that had a happy ending. Who knows where this will lead? I consider walking out while I still have the chance. Haven't I given it enough time? Maybe I should get up right now, and split. What about *my* welfare? A moment later, Nicki finally opens her eyes.

"I don't wanna keep living like this," she whispers, more clear-headed than before.

Hope jumps in my heart. "Honey, you don't have to. You can get help."

"Help where?" she says. "Who?"

"They have programs. Nicki. You can do it. You're just going through a hard spot."

"But it's *always* hard. It *never* gets easier." Her voice is getting shrill now.

"You need professional help. You're so damn depressed and you're making me depressed. How many times do I have to tell you? Nicki, I can't take this." She starts crying.

"I hate life," she yells at me. "I hate this fucking life." She pounds her pillow with a fist.

"You hate life? Do you hate me?"

"No!"

"Do you hate what we have?"

"I love us," she says clearly.

"Well then, shit, Nicki. Get some help. You're drinking your life away. Goddammit. I love you, but what am I supposed to do?" I shout through my tears. "You keep putting me in this position because you know I love you. And I do. But doesn't that count for anything? Doesn't it make a difference?"

"It does," she says, drifting off to sleep. "It *really* does." Her eyes are closing again, and I'm left sitting there, on the edge of the bed, wondering if I can possibly believe her.

Last Bus Home

Bethia Rayne

Sweat trickled down Henry's back as she powered along Elizabeth Street. Her breath rasped in her throat as she dragged her fingers unconsciously through her hair; those passing instinctively gave her a wide berth. Henry was oblivious to all of them, the urgency of her thoughts pushing her on faster. She had to get there in time. Once Cassie left London, she'd have lost her for good.

At the coach station, Henry looked about her carefully before approaching a small booth with an open window near the entrance hall.

"Where does the last bus to Glasgow leave from?" she asked the guard. Her voice was soft, at odds with her appearance: scuffed leather jacket, baggy, patched jeans, worn army boots and spiky green hair. The guard looked at her with tired disapproval. "Down there, Platform 5, due to depart any minute."

Henry backed from him and started to track the platform numbers with her eyes; her pupils dilated as Cassie's long, curly hair entered her line of vision. Henry moved closer with the stealth of a predator, her earlier apprehension replaced with a steady calm. She slipped her arm around Cassie's shoulders and looked down intently into her heart-shaped face. "I want to take you somewhere we can talk."

"It's too late, Henry," Cassie said. "I've phoned Mum and told her I'm coming home, she'll be waiting up for me. Anyway Sandie's thrown me out, that cold-hearted bitch." Her voice was shaking.

Henry slipped her fingers down the velvet collar of Cassie's jacket, massaging the delicate curve of her neck in a gentle, circular rhythm. "Come on, sweetie, give your Mum a call," Henry said. "Tell her you're okay now."

"But I've got nowhere to stay."

Henry smiled, sensing a weakening in Cassie's resolve. She bent down and picked up the two small canvas bags in one hand with such ease a casual observer would have believed they were empty.

"Please, Cassie, don't leave me," she said. Tracing Cassie's cheekbone with her fist, Henry held Cassie's gaze, saw the amber eyes and sullen mouth in her pale face. She then drew her fist down under Cassie's chin, tilting her face towards her, and slowly kissed her soft, cherry-flavored mouth. She sucked Cassie's underlip before sliding her tongue into her mouth, entering the hot, moist cavern beyond in a deep intimate kiss. "I know you've been through a lot recently, but I'm going to take care of you now," Henry said. She slipped her free hand into Cassie's, then oblivious to the disapproving stares of others, they turned and walked from the bus terminal to the payphones and the District Line.

Henry leaned back on the dingy, tweed-covered seats of the tube running her fingers along the top of the seat but not touching Cassie, who wriggled about seemingly uncomfortable at her side. Henry could smell the hot, cloying scent of Cassie's arousal; her smile caused the passenger opposite to return hurriedly to her book. "I'll get you a place I know just beside Ravenscourt Park, it'll be ideal," Henry said, then pressed her forefinger to Cassie's lips before she could protest. "You're worth it, sweetie."

Cassie's gaze took in the luxury of the hotel room: the large, metal-framed bed, the lush, grey carpet, the heavy, silk drapes. Henry dropped the bags into the bottom of the wardrobe and then, from the depths of her jacket pocket, she removed a small-handled whip with a thick, knotted, leather thong and placed it onto one of the many satin pillows on the bed. Cassie watched, licking her lips as if they had suddenly become unbearably dry. Henry then went into the bathroom and started running the taps; she smelled the contents of three small bottles of bath foam supplied by the hotel and then poured them all under the stream of hot water. The steam in the bathroom became aromatic with the scent of roses and gardenias. Henry sat on the edge of the bath, one booted foot resting on the rim, studying Cassie as she undressed: the creamy, voluptuous curves; the heavy breasts, their dark aureoles already hard and distended; the soft, golden hairs which protected her pussy that were now moist and forming into small curls. Cassie, catching Henry's eyes with her own, walked slowly into the bathroom and stood in front of her. Henry turned off the taps and, turning, pressed her warm, damp hands against Cassie's peachy buttocks, drawing her between her legs. Henry slowly traced the lace edge of the coffee-colored hold-ups Cassie always wore, causing her to part her legs and arch her slick sex downwards; then Henry, giving Cassie's engorged clitoris the lightest brush with her fingertips, stood up and cupped Cassie's face with her hands, pressing her parted lips against Cassie's cheek and then tracing the line of her jaw with her tongue to the small hollow behind her ear. "You'll not be running away again, Cassie," Henry whispered, "I don't like to be put to so much inconvenience in one day, it tries my patience."

Cassie began to tremble. She opened her mouth to plead, but was stopped by a gentle fist placed over her lips.

"Let's not discuss this anymore. It's over and there's no time," Henry said, rising. "Your trick will be here soon and she's paid exceptionally well for the privilege of whipping your plumb arse. Your percentage will be very good – as always."

Echoes of Her Voice

Anya Levin

Her day had been horrible, and the simple act of coming home to a dark, cold apartment had her almost in tears. All she wanted was to hear Venetia tell her, in that sexy voice, that everything was going to be alright. She was getting wet already, just thinking about it. She debated calling. Venetia didn't have to know that she was masturbating while she talked.

Therese would understand, she knew. It was yet another part of having your best friend take up with the lover you discarded. The threesome had been her idea, after all. "No hard feelings," she had said with a smile. "I want you too."

Words that had shaken Tricia's world.

The phone number was programmed into auto-dial, so all she had to do was press 'three.' She had called too many times, and she knew it.

Therese answered the phone. "Is Venetia there?" Tricia asked.

"Ah, Tricia! It's been a while since you've called. I thought you'd decided not to talk to us anymore." Though sexy in a husky way, her flat-voweled American voice chilled Tricia.

"Please, is Venetia there?"

Therese went to fetch Venetia. "Hello, Tricia," Venetia said warmly.

Tricia squeezed her eyes shut, shuddering with pleasure at hearing the tone of her voice. "Speak to me," she said. "Just talk to me."

"You've had a bad day, darling?" Her accent made the question sound almost dangerous. "You know you're welcome to come over. Anytime."

The offer was – as always – tempting. "Too many strings," she reminded Venetia.

"A girl has to try," she crooned.

"Please," Tricia managed.

Even Venetia's laugh was enough to send skitters of pleasure down her spine.

"Are you naked yet?" Venetia asked.

Tricia swallowed. Of course she knew. She had always known before, why would she not know this time?

"Not yet."

"Take off your clothes," Venetia instructed.

Trembling, Tricia obeyed. Her panties snagged on her leg and she had to tug them down.

"Have you undressed?"

"Yes."

"Touch yourself."

Her fingers slid downward. With a great inhalation, she touched the heat of her wetness. Her clit throbbed beneath her touch.

"Are you wet?"

"Very," Tricia breathed.

"Put your finger in your cunt," Venetia said.

Tricia sighed at the way she said "cunt." The word echoed in her mind as she slid her finger home.

Venetia laughed. "I heard that," she said. "You're really wet, aren't you? You should come over and let me lick you."

Tricia groaned. "I can't, and you know it. Stop torturing me."

"I like torturing you," Venetia said. "Bien. As you say."

Tricia felt the walls of her cunt grip her fingers. "Venetia. . . ."

"Oui? You love my voice, non? You love to hear me speak to you."

"Yes." Her fingers were flying now, dancing across her clit. The phone was clenched against her shoulder. "More," she said, gritting her teeth.

"Quoi?"

Tricia moaned into the phone. Her harsh breathing was reflected back at her, coated with the metallic edge of distance.

"Cherie," Venetia breathed. "I want to see you."

"Aah . . . yes. . . ." Tricia thrust her fingers in deeply, groaning at the sensation that shot through her hips and pebbled her nipples.

"Tricia," Venetia said, her own breath ragged. Tricia wondered, was she masturbating too? The thought was too much. With a loud cry, Tricia came.

Venetia whispered in her ear as the shudders wound to an end. Slowly, with exquisite care, Tricia pulled her fingers from her sopping cunt. She wiped them on a towel, the phone still clutched to her ear. Venetia's low cries confirmed her activities. Tricia closed her eyes at the sounds of her orgasm.

"Are you good now?" Venetia asked.

Was she? Tricia sniffed. "Yes, I'm fine. Do you . . . do you want me to explain to Therese?"

"No, it's all right," Venetia said. Tricia could almost see her Gallic shrug. "She understands these things."

Tricia hung up the phone slowly. How could Therese understand? *She* didn't understand.

She dressed hurriedly, pulling on her damp panties and fastening her pants as fast as she could. She started to put on her shirt, and then shivered.

With one touch she erased the speed dial.

Never again.

She turned off the light, itching to take a shower, to be beneath the cleansing flow of the water. She glanced back at the phone. She could still hear the echoes of her voice.

Anger

Barbara Brown

It's early. I can't sleep. Pain fills my body, taking me back to the abuse. Age six. Powerless. I am so angry I can't move. Can't breathe. This is how I've known anger all my life. My body longs to scream or tremble, but I don't dare: make no noise, make no movements, and soon it will all be over. I learned my lesson young. The trigger was insignificant. My foot caught in the sheets as I rolled over, wanting to hold Sandra laying here beside me. My leg, trapped momentarily, has created this paralyzing vigilance.

Holding it in, I wait for the anger to pass, but it doesn't. Instead, the tension of my rage ripples uncontrollably through my body, down into my cunt. Sandra is stirring, little movements of testing. She knows something is up. She recognizes the signs of my anger. Sandra knows to leave me alone. But she also feels me shudder.

Sandra turns, looking into me with unrelenting compassion. I won't return her gaze. Her penetrating watch, intense heat of being seen, tips me further into the place I've been longing to go. She rolls away, opens the drawer to her bedside table and, rolling back, leans the full weight of her lithe body against mine. Her athlete's muscles feel hard against my still, stiff pose.

"It's going to be different this time," she says softly, and slides her hand full of gel down my pyjama bottoms.

I don't move.

"It's going to get better," she says with tender certainty. I don't breathe. Smearing my clit and my mound she begins slowly, gently rubbing.

"Spread your legs," she whispers into my ear.

"I'm not ready."

"When you're ready," she says, slipping her tongue along my ear, my chin, my neck.

She now hovers above me, her legs spread to straddle me. Her morning scent is musky and strong, and fills my quickening breath. I can feel that she's hot already. One of her hands never stops circling, round and round my clit. The other pulls up my shirt to expose my breasts. She wraps her mouth around my nipple and begins sucking.

Desire mixes with anger as my legs of their own accord begin to spread open, pressing against the inside of her muscled thighs. Her teeth graze my nipple; her tongue wets my breast. She sucks. She circles. The tension begins to fall away, propelling me onward. I push harder at her legs until one moves, allowing me space to expose my cunt, now dripping with my own lube. She knows what I want, knows that I'm ready, and she's there. Strapped on. Pushing, sliding, entering me. Touching me inside, in a place I didn't know needed her, the place that's held my anger. This place quivering itself loose, letting go. Circling over my clit harder, my hips rise to meet her, to pull her in. The pain disappears.

"Don't let me go. Keep me close. Please."

And I come. And she stays in me. Quiet. Still. Near. I move. Drawing myself to her with each easing contraction, I scream.

I breathe.

Sandra rests her weight softly on top of me, our pyjamas pushed into bunches around our feet. The smell of our sweaty bodies infuses the room. She kisses me on my lips, a waking-up morning kiss, and in response my cunt grabs at the silicone dick inside me, final reverberation of an unexpected orgasm. She falls asleep. I lay awake, my arms around her. There is a calm inside. No resistance. I am ready to stand up for my six-year-old self.

I am still angry. Fiercely angry.

Through the Secret Passage

Miriam Carroll

Far below the lonely castle at the edge of the world, the sea ebbed. Hidden in the gloom of the darkening mist, a small rowboat pulled up against the rock-bound cliff, locating the exact spot where an immense cave yawned open. It was accessible only at low tide, and impossible to locate by sight from the sea. The lithe form at the oar pulled into the dark recess, and tied up at an ancient iron staple embedded in the rock ledge. The figure nimbly jumped to the slippery shelf, then groped along to a massive oaken door. Thrice the knocker sounded, echoing along the cavern. At last, the door creaked open. A voice familiar to the guest whispered, "It's about time, you. Mother Superior Positionatus does not like to be kept waiting."

Another dark shape, whose face was lit by a flaming torch, urged the juvenile forward. Shaking off the dampness, the newcomer flung back a woolen cap, revealing a mess of unkempt flaxen hair.

The two elder nuns said not another word, but hastened along the dank tunnel which still stank of ancient battles against pirates and invaders of ancient days. Finally, the group emerged into the cold night air.

"Hurry, Sister, as the dogs will sound the alarum in a moment," hissed the tall black-shrouded nun, hauling the short one by the elbow along a rutted path, through the ghost-filled family cemetery, crossing themselves on the way, muttering the proper incantations. Their destination was the small chapel, where, 'twas rumored, the bones of the first nobles and their gold were interred beneath the stone floor. Their destination was the nuns' quarters, a private building on the hallowed grounds. The tall nun knocked on an inner door.

"Enter, and let us see whom you have brought to amuse us the night," cackled the elderly nun who appeared in the doorway. A fine fire in the hearth dispelled the gloom and chill.

The sister pushed the young one forward.

"Ah, 'tis Peter Paula, I see. Rather, let us all see this marvelous anomaly. Quickly now, the tide awaits no man. Or woman, as the case may be here. Here, Peter Paula, let me help you remove that cassock," gloated the queenly Mum. "Sister Virginia Monologia, please call our novice, Sister Abby Unabashed. She must have her initiation rites tonight."

Sister Virginia scurried off, returning a moment later with Sister Abby Unabashed, who was thrilled to be in at last on the secret comings and goings of the older nuns, who always seemed so starry-eyed after a trip to Mother's quarters. Surely she would see God tonight!

Mother Superior Positionatus whipped off the youth's shapeless garment. The others drew back in wonder and delight. No matter how often Peter Paula visited, it was always a thrill, for they could never believe their eyes! The body had breasts, topped by pretty pink coronas and crowned with nipples, as extended as the lovely Johnson dangling lustily between his thighs.

Peter Paula blushed, yet made no attempt to cover the appendage, which began to waggle enticingly. Giggles and gasps erupted from the clutch of sisters, but young Sister Abby Unabashed just stared.

"Never saw anything like that awful thing in my life," she said in a long, drawn out whisper.

"I'm going to have the operation as soon as I can afford it, and your gaping will come to an end," Peter Paula sniveled, "and I expect to be paid two gold sovereigns for your viewing pleasure tonight."

"And a bit of touch for such a price, eh?" bargained Mother Superior Positionatus.

"Then let's get to it," mocked Peter Paula, "Off with your own shmatas and let's all have a look." The manly half was now in charge.

Peter Paula's voice echoed through the stone vault, through hidden halls beneath the ground and secret passageways that led to the main castle, where the lord and lady disported themselves, intent on every whisper.

"Ooh! They're having another party! Let's hurry down the back way and have a look, too," said Lady Glenclosier.

"Great idea," concurred her handsome, virile young Lord St John Malkontent. "Maybe that wicked Mother Superior Positionatus will amuse the lad – or is it lass? – with some new tricks for us to practice, and it won't cost us a ha'penny."

With that, the two hastened through a secret closet to their private lookie-hole.

Meanwhile, in the large chamber, without a moment's hesitation, everyone's garments flew off. As undergarments were a thing of the future, bare flesh brought forth coos of delight at the sight of warm breasts which had never known binding, and curvy buttocks rarely knowing a touch, except perhaps for the saintly kiss of a penitential switch by the owner's own hand.

Tentative pats and gentle kisses led to desire, which led to the sweet-smelling bower of hay thoughtfully prepared by Mother Superior Positionatus. Moments later, one could scarcely tell who belonged to what leg, arm, or head which was enmeshed on whomsoever's nether parts. Delightful sucking sounds, gasps, and moans ensued.

How quickly does young Sister Unabashed learn the ways to ecstasy, thought Mother Superior Positionatus, diving deeper into someone's furry patch as her own flow ran like the seas itself.

"I feel the intense religious experience I've always longed for," shrieked Sister Abby Unabashed, whose head appeared above the melee. "It's upon me! Oh, sweet Jesus! I am arriving! Yes!" and fell back in a swoon for more religious experience.

► ► ►

Outside the castle, the sea pushed forward in its never-ending routine, helping the aspiring novice row home. The exhausted Halfling, now two coins closer to joining her sisters in their solemn vows of chastity, relished the gold sovereigns safe in his pocket.

Instruction of Faith

Elizabeth Roue

"Get up, miss! Your bath is ready and you must be downstairs in two hours."

Molly flung open the curtains and turned to prod the languid figure still draped across the bed. Creamy skin peeped through folds of a casually wrapped robe. As the girl wriggled in protest, the wrappings fell even farther apart, revealing perfect round globes tipped in pale pink, and a fine mist of golden hair over the cleft of her sex.

She grasped the arm the girl lazily held out to her and pulled the reluctant nymph from the bed, catching her close before she stumbled. Molly's breathing quickened, and she felt a familiar tightening in her quim as the firm, lush body pressed against her own.

"Come on, miss." Molly stepped back to hold the girl at arm's length. "Time for your bath."

Faith pouted and watched Molly as the young maid prepared Faith's evening attire, her slim body bent gracefully over the bed. Faith watched with interest as Molly's breasts strained against the fabric of the cheap uniforms her mother supplied. She'd obviously been given a uniform cast down from a maid with much smaller charms. Now and again breasts threatened to spill out the top.

Faith did not resist as Molly led her to the large steaming tub in the dressing room. Dropping the robe carelessly from her shoulders, she peeped over her shoulder to note with satisfaction Molly's eyes wandering down the length of her body. Finally, with a soft moan of pleasure, Faith lowered herself into the warm, fragrant water.

Molly tore her eyes from the sight of the rosy nipples bobbing in the water. "Will that be all, miss?"

"No, Molly, stay and wash my back." Faith sat up, holding out a washcloth. "There is something I need to talk to you about."

Confused, Molly took the cloth and gently began to stroke Faith's slender back. "What is it, miss?"

"You know my father means to marry me to one of the suitable young men he's been bringing around. Lord this, Lord that. Good lord, I'm tired of it!"

Molly giggled in sympathy. "Aye, miss, but you know you must do your duty."

"That's right. Duty." Faith leaned back against the tub, reaching up to grasp Molly's hand before she could pull it away. Their hands rested together on top of Faith's shoulder, water from the cloth streaming over her breasts. Molly kept an eye on the water tricking down, watching its journey.

"I know what my duty is," Faith continued, "and I know what my duty will be come the wedding night. I know, but I don't really *know*. I want you to show me."

Panic bloomed in Molly's chest. "What do you mean, miss?"

Faith turned to face Molly, skin flushed rosy from the warm water. "I want you to show me what love-making feels like."

Molly stepped back slowly. "I can't do that, miss. Surely you must understand that."

"I don't understand. I want to know. I want you to show me, or else —" She looked at Molly sternly. "Or else I will have you dismissed."

All of a sudden Molly felt both fear and excitement coursing through her veins. For a year now she'd been watching this young lady dress, undress, and bathe, and the sight of her blooming body never failed to excite her. There were days when Molly's thighs would be slick with desire under her skirts while doing her duties, and now, Faith was offering her body freely. Molly felt her breasts swelling under her bodice, juice running down her thighs.

"As you wish, miss."

Faith leaned back into the bath, her eyes closed. Molly grasped the washcloth with a shaking hand and gently started stroking the fine skin along Faith's neck. She leaned forward until Faith's head was cradled against her breasts. The cloth dipped downward into the water, circling one perfect mound, then the other.

Faith arched slightly, thrusting her breasts out of the water. Her breathing deepened as the cloth rubbed first one nipple, then the other, into hard pink points. Molly abandoned the cloth and curved her hands around Faith, cradling her breasts in wet palms and caressing the waiting nipples between teasing fingertips.

Faith's breathing became more urgent as she pushed her throbbing breasts harder and harder into Molly's hands. She turned her head and moaned into Molly's neck. At the touch of Faith's lips, Molly's head turned in response. Molly lowered her mouth onto the soft lips she'd been yearning for. Their lips met, tongues tentative, then hungry, dipping, tasting.

When their lips finally parted, some shred of sense worked its way into Molly's head. Releasing Faith, she gently but firmly lowered the flushed girl back into the water. "We . . . we must get you ready, miss. We're running out of time."

Faith slapped the water petulantly. "Not yet! I want more."

Hiding the smile that lurked behind her firm lips, Molly shook her head decisively. "No, miss. If we don't hurry, your mother will be along to see what the delay is." She paused thoughtfully. "However, miss, remember I'll be here to help you get ready for bed later tonight."

Faith hesitated, then nodded. She rose out of the water imperiously and stood while Molly gently patted her dry with a thick towel. Molly noted how Faith shuddered slightly when the towel passed over her tender nipples. Molly could scarcely control herself as she dried Faith's long, slender legs. Kneeling before her, gazing at the silken hair covering the ripe, split mound, Molly felt a fierce urge to bury her tongue deep inside, to taste the sweet juice and feel Faith buckle against her.

Instinctively, Faith opened her thighs slightly. She reached down with a hesitant hand and stroked the top of Molly's head. Molly looked up, her face as flushed as Faith's. Taking a deep breath, she gave Faith's thighs a final pat.

"I'll get your dress, miss."

The Twins

Anh-Thu Huynh

BA ME THUOC, VIETNAM, FRIDAY JUNE 14, 1972

Sister Margaret was beside herself again. She was furious with the twins. The wretched, debauched orphans. Brown eyes, stony cheeks. Dark brown skin, had never seen a day of shade. She made them bend over her desk and drop their panties for all to see. "Skipping class three times this week? Shame, shame, shame," she screamed, flogging their tiny behinds to a pulp. From where she stood, shame and pain went well together. Red and brown welts on bare buttocks, new overlapping old, criss-crossing the clenched brown anuses. A sight for sore eyes.

The thin bamboo stick kept coming. The girls clenched their teeth, kept it all in. No tears, no sobs, no regrets. Soon, Sister Margaret would send them to detention to pray with Sister Agatha. There, Sister Agatha would hold their faces to her sweet bosoms, where they would cry aloud, and cling for love the way orphanage girls would. Then, they would stick out their buttocks, show off their wounds, gleaming under her teary eyes. Trembling hands. What orphans wouldn't do for gratuitous love?

The torn bamboo stick kept striking. The girls hung on to her desk, wobbled their knees. Numbed from pain, they could almost smell Sister Agatha's tenderness. Soon, she would soothe their wounds with her gingerly touch, wash their lesions with her tears, cure their pain with forgiving kisses. There, they would squirm when she'd rub the sticky ointment all over. What adolescents wouldn't do for forbidden pleasure?

The third time this week, Sister Agatha was furious with herself. The lure of the twins, identical and wretched. Big eyes, big lips. The soft, supple, Asian skin. Alone at night, a thin bamboo stick, she flogged herself. "Caressing orphans three times this week. Shame, shame, shame," she whimpered, striking again and again. From where she knelt, guilt and pain belonged together. Brown and red welts on her bare chest, old overlapping new, criss-crossing the oozing rosy nipples. A sight for sore eyes.

Dr Barrett Closes

Claudia Berty

"Ready?" she asks impatiently. The anaesthetist nods. In one deft movement her scalpel flashes a thin smile four inches long just above the patient's pubic hairline. Blood starts to bead along the cut, but before she can ask, I staunch the flow with a large white swab of gauze. I am assisting, and it's my job to read the surgeon's mind and to anticipate her every move.

Down and down, the dissection continues. I mop, I burn, I tie off vessels, I follow barked instructions. Layers peel back until we are staring at the woman's core. Her uterus, ovaries, and fallopian tubes gleam under the blanching lights of the operating theater. Inside, the colors are beautiful; mainly reds, blues, and yellows. Nobody tells you how vivid yellow human fat is, strangely artificial, body technicolor at its best.

TAH. Total Abdominal Hysterectomy. We tie off and detach the woman's reproductive life. Plop. It is contained in a stainless steel bowl. I stare at Dr Forrester. She is concentrating. Her short brown hair is tucked under her theater cap, but a few spikes stick out. She is lean and wiry, her fingers long and thin. Like a spider, they scuttle nimbly, leaving a web of black, green, and purple threads in their wake. Her brown eyes flit and scan. She is intense, talented, and frankly gorgeous.

Electricity jolts me. Have I touched the diathermy by mistake? No, our hands have touched inside the shell of pelvis. We are both wearing surgical gloves, so the touch is intimate but unsatisfying. "Move your hand," she barks. I look up. Only our eyes are visible above our surgical masks, and I can feel my face growing hot and red beneath mine. Between my legs it's pretty hot, too. Am I wet? My body is sweaty under my green surgical gown. My clit is throbbing and I'm losing my concentration.

"Are you okay?" she asks, although she doesn't really care what my answer is.

"Yes," I manage, even though my mouth, unlike the rest of my moist body, has dried up.

"Close for me then, Dr Barrett," she commands. Before I can answer, she has snapped off her gloves, the scrub nurse has untied her gown at the back, and she is gone.

As the only remaining surgeon, I check the field and begin to close. I stitch muscle and fat, and then close the skin. I could use staples as they are quick and efficient, but instead decide to use a subcuticular stitch which runs just under the skin and leaves a thinner, more cosmetically pleasing scar. I am pleased with the results and thank the team for their work before I scrub out and head for the changing room.

What a relief to be free from the theater wear. My soft blue cotton scrubs are wet under the arms, between my breasts, down my back, and between my legs. I breathe in my own scent and then exhale forcefully, still excited from my encounter with Dr Forrester and just from being in theater. I need a cool drink of water, a pee, and a warm shower after a hard afternoon's work. And I still need to calm down. My friends tease me about the high level of testosterone floating around in theater and its effect on me, but it's no joke, really. It makes me hot.

So, I'm considering masturbating in the changing room and smile to myself as I strip off my top and empty my pockets. As I look for a clean towel, Dr Forrester emerges from the bathroom. We both freeze. What the hell is she still doing here? She is fucking butt naked and it takes my breath away. Her body is slim and brown, with flat breasts, muscular legs, and a slightly round belly.

Defiant, nonplussed by the fact that she has no clothes on and that my nipples are pointing at her almost accusingly, she neither moves away nor recoils. The tension mounts. I take a step forward – maybe towards her, maybe towards the shower – and her eyes look brighter; her expression softens. All of a sudden, I know instinctively that this bitch, this cold, dominating surgeon wants it, and she wants me to take over. She has wanted it since the first day we strode past each other in the hospital corridor and her eyes held mine just a nanosecond too long.

I take a chance – probably one of the biggest I've taken in my life – and I move close to her, forcing her to step into the shower room. I push her so that her own back is holding the door shut. My face presses so close to hers that our noses touch, and I can feel her breath and her eyelashes on my face. We linger there before I start to kiss her. To my surprise, she kisses me back, our tongues deep and probing. I can't quite believe this is happening and I can't decide which part of her body to get into my mouth first, so I kiss her neck and move quickly on to her breasts and her stomach.

She is so receptive to my touch, it's like an electrical current as my lips trace down to her lush mound. I part her pubic hair with my tongue, seeking out her sweet clit, or the bit that will make her moan and writhe and cover my face with her wetness.

I hold her up against the door physically as she starts to collapse onto me, muscular legs no good to her now, as my tongue laps and circles and she holds onto my hair. As her moans subside, her body starts to relax. She comes up to meet my mouth for more kisses and we both begin to giggle.

"Close for me now, Dr Forrester!" I command, and I know she'll do exactly what I want.

Strangers

Mar Stevens

It's a Friday night and I am walking the streets of San Francisco. It's an un-usually warm night in the city and I'm loving it. People are out, the noise level is high, and the pace is fast. I'm feeling really happy and kind of sexy as I move through the streets. I'm feeling free.

I arrive at Labadi, the women's bathhouse, and ring the doorbell. A cute woman answers the door smiling, wearing a skirt and big black boots. I pay my fee and enter the locker room. Nude women stroll casually about; some are getting dressed. I can feel my shyness come over me, but also my desires. I undress, shower, then head for the hot tub. As I push open the door, I imme-diately hear voices, which stop when I enter. The room is big and dimly lit.

The warm outside air fills the room from the open back door that leads to the saunas. The floor is damp and cool on my feet. There are five women in the hot tub and all eyes are on me as I step in. The sensation of the hot water over my body turns me on immediately. I feel my nipples getting hard. I glance over and notice a sign reading "Sexual activity is not allowed." I wonder how often this rule is broken? I sit back with my eyes closed, letting the hot water relax me. Casually, I look up to notice the woman across from me gazing over my body, which is exposed from the waist up. As my stare meets hers, she smiles, lowering her eyes to my breasts. I look down; my nipples are standing at attention. I shyly smile back, low-ering my body further into the tub. She teasingly gives me a disappointed look. I can tell she liked the view.

She is beautiful. Her skin is a golden brown, her eyes are dark, and her dreadlocks are long and tied back. She nods toward the back door as she stands and steps out of the tub, water trickling off her naked body. She is strong and luscious. I study her curves from the back as she reaches for her towel. She knows I am watching her and gives me another glance as she heads for the outside area.

I wait a minute before I get out of the hot tub. Her flirty eyes have stimulated every nerve in my body. She has aroused me completely and I am feeling horny, ready to fuck. I walk outside and see two saunas, the first of which looks unoccupied. I open the door of the second one and find her there, sitting back with her eyes closed. She opens them and smiles as she watches me enter. I position my towel on the seat with my back to her. My tight ass is in her face as I swing around and sit across from her.

She lays back, her eyes still on me. She closes her eyes and opens her legs, slowly unfolding her pussy in front of me. Sweat drips from her bush, which she pulls back, exposing her clitoris. Not saying a word, she starts rubbing her clit while moving her hips in a circular motion. Her pussy is big and her clit is swollen. I want to get on my knees to feel her hardness on my mouth, my tongue. My pussy is dripping and the heat from the sauna is making me sweat. I want to serve her. I know I can even though we are in a public place. I'm paralyzed, watching her every move. She moves her finger from her clit and inserts her thumb into her pussy. The sweat pours off of her body as she continues to grind herself. My body is now covered in salty wet droplets. My mouth aches to taste her. The pain in my pussy is so intense I can feel the juices drip. We still are not speaking, but our eyes lock and I know what she wants.

I kneel in front of her and she removes her thumb from her pussy, spreading her legs wider. I know she can take all that I can give. I enter her with two fingers, then slide my entire hand inside as I form a fist. She moans silently as I start to fist fuck her. This woman is hot and her vagina walls open wider as my fist pounds into her. I am fucking both her and myself, as I rub my own swollen clit. We are total strangers dripping in sweat and not saying a word to each other. We are in rhythm with every thrust and now I'm coming and so is she. I feel her pussy clamp down hard on my fist, causing my own pussy to jerk. I move my finger from my clit, and penetrate my vagina while fisting her one last time. Her pussy is powerful, as is mine. We come fast and hard. Her vagina grips my fist as it releases. She's warm inside and I feel her juices slide down my arm just as my own douses my fingers. She's beautiful laying back, glistening. I don't move and neither does she, as we stare at each other. We are two strangers, holding on to the moment, in silence.

Chopped Liver

Shari J. Berman

"And a small chopped liver?"

She looked up as if seeing me for the very first time. "Yes. How did you know?"

"ESP," I lied. She came in every time she was troubled and always ordered the same things: half a pound of nova lox, half a pound of lean pastrami, two poppy seed bagels and two bialys, half a pound of new pickles, a seeded rye bread, and a small chopped liver. I had it memorized, along with every line on her face. She was drop-dead gorgeous. I'd have been happy to offer her some cozy alternative to her regular depression-deli-to-go, but she was more than likely straight.

"What's your name?" she asked.

Damn. We were not following the script today. I removed my gloves to ring her up. "Eve."

"Chava? Me, too . . . my English name is Holly, but my Jewish name is Chava. Holly Simon," she finished, offering her hand over the cash register. I shook it, desperately trying not to swallow loudly.

I know your name. I've run your credit card through many times. To wallow in a cliché, I had always been some extension of the chopped liver to her before. How had I suddenly come to life? Was predicting her order such an amazing party trick? Suddenly, I was overcome with diffidence. I checked my apron for ugly food stains.

She was gone, but I could still detect the aroma of her apricot-scented hand lotion beyond the salmon and whitefish odor that permeated my clothes. Holly and her apricot essence provided a momentary fantasy.

Manny Gould lifted me from my reverie ordering some belly lox. I replaced my gloves and carved carefully. It doesn't require years of apprenticeship like a sushi chef, but there is skill to delicatessen fish slicing.

"Nice and thin, *madele*," Manny admonished.

"It's thin, Manny, look. And I haven't been a *madele* since ten years before your last cataract surgery." We laughed. Manny was typical of the clientele – an old guy whose language was peppered with Yiddish. In Manny's defense, I was a young girl the first time he walked in. Sol, my dad, would have been slicing the lox and my mother, Yetta, running the register. Now, I do both while my parents flit to early bird specials in Boca Raton.

After a year of puking my guts out trying to pretend I could stand the pressure and the sight of blood in med school, I had returned to the deli. My mother was semi-retired at the time. She'd come and play mah jong on Monday afternoons at the dining tables with friends. Her favorite joke was, "Evie thought we said 'you should work with sturgeons,' not 'surgeons,' so she quit medical school." Maybe that was humorous the first dozen times – I can't remember.

Holly continued to come in regularly, getting her usual order. She always made eye contact with me, even smiled, but there was a haunting sadness about her. I sensed she wanted to say something yet didn't. Neither did I. The dreams I had about her surely would have sent her running.

She dropped in one Friday for a traditional Sabbath *challah*. She was surprisingly chipper. Mind you, I never took the dim moods personally. I figured she ate Italian when she was in a good mood and deli when she wasn't. She then stayed away for the next two weeks until I was called to the phone.

"Eve?"

"Yes?"

"It's Holly Simon. Could you deliver an order?"

"Sure."

"I want a half –"

I decided to save us time and told her exactly what I knew she wanted. My clairvoyance was working. I usually had someone else handle deliveries, but it was an hour before closing. I left that to the dining room manager and headed to Holly's.

She looked even more miserable than she usually did placing her depressed-and-desiring-deli order. I offered to put the cold stuff away, leaving her huddled on the sofa in a pink robe with that too-bummed-to-get-dressed look.

Refrigerators tell tales – Holly lived alone. At least whoever made her miserable was not cohabitating.

I started to excuse myself when she said, "Sit down . . . please."

I slumped into the armchair next to the sofa. "What's wrong, Holly?"

Through choked sobs, she said, "Terry dumped me . . . for good."

"Terry's a total jerk," I blurted out, not checking with my brain.

"She said you'd say that."

"She? It's a she? And she talked about me?" I paused to collect my thoughts. "And here I thought I was just chopped liver."

Holly managed a chuckle as she swiped at her tears. Her laughter sounded like soft rain. I had enough adrenaline to lift the sofa up with her on it, but instead I took her in my arms.

I kissed her gently, but her tongue probed with dire urgency. *Damn.* I lost the will to be good. I wouldn't be her first woman, just her best. I opened the robe to reveal two perfect pale breasts the shape of our finest potato *knishes.* Wrapping my lips around a nipple, I proceeded to ignite a fire.

No undergarments in my way, I brushed my fingers across her silky mound; there was little doubt that she was ready. "Eve needs to taste the forbidden fruit," I whispered.

Then, I positioned her on the armchair and drew her legs up. I stood behind the chair and ministered to her; her head lolled over the edge.

She came with a spectacular shudder; then I pulled her against me. We spent the rest of the night making love. In the morning, her face was resting against mine and she whispered, "Foie gras, sweetie. That's what you are."

Chopped liver, indeed.

The Question

Michelle Bouché

"How does that make you feel?"

It was one of her favorite questions. Made sense, I suppose, she *is* my therapist after all. Still, I squirm whenever she asks. I make stuff up. Sad, anxious, whatever I think would make some logical sense along with the other lies I tell her. For I have a dirty little secret that she'll never know. Because how I feel is hot. Horny, wet down there, where your mom said not to touch. And I can't tell her because she's the one making me feel that way.

Oh, I know, everyone's supposed to fall in love with their therapist. There's some fancy name for it. You work out your problems through your relationship with your shrink. Well, maybe that's how it started, me falling into the same trap that everyone else goes through.

But it doesn't feel like therapy anymore. It hasn't since I noticed that she was starting to dress up for me. Oh, it was just little things, a new scarf, maybe an extra dab of perfume. But I knew it was for me. And it got me hot. It got me even hotter because I know she's straight. She has her wedding picture on her desk. Somehow, her orientation made it all the more tantalizing. It means that I had worked my magic on her and she was noticing me noticing back. Maybe she wasn't even aware of it. Maybe she was deluding herself that the extra fragrance smeared between her swelling breasts was just to give her a little extra lift. I wonder what fantasies she told *her* therapist.

Normally, I like my women stick thin, little buds for breasts, sharp hipbones that poke out and leave bruises on me when we make love. Doctor Angela is nothing like that. She's voluptuous, round, curvy; a big woman, her flesh ripples all over whenever she moves. Still, she's graceful when she floats into her office. Sometimes I sit biting my lip, watching the swell of her calf when she crosses her legs, wanting her to move just a bit so that her dress exposes more of her succulent thighs. I imagine what it would be like to slip my hand up under that lace, the skirt an open invitation to her treasure beneath.

"How does that make you feel?"

I hardly remember what we've been talking about. Any problems I had when we started this have long since gone, especially after she told me to start taking better care of myself. I do that every week, when I jack-off to fantasies of her.

No, the only problem I have now is when she asks me that question. I want to show her how it makes me feel. I want to turn the tables on her. I want to kiss her, part her lips with my tongue, and penetrate her deeply. I want to loosen the front of her dress and take hold of one of those large, luscious nipples, pinching it between my fingers before I pop it into my mouth, sucking it into the hardness of a diamond. I want to expose her other nipple and torment it with my tongue, then trace the path up her legs and slip my fingers into the wetness between those juicy thighs. Then it would be my turn to ask, "How does that make you feel?"

But I would already know. Because she would be moaning, breathing so heavily that her breasts would be bobbing up and down in front of my face.

"Yes," she would say. "Touch me there."

And I would oblige because it makes me hot to know how much she is enjoying it, how much she wants it. Except . . . then I pull back, withholding some, making her ask.

"Please," she would say. "Please, more. I've thought about this so long. It's been so hard to see you every week, sitting on my couch and not touching you, not having you touch me. *Please. . . .*"

That's all it would take. Then I would move down to my knees in front of her, pushing those mighty thighs wide open, unlocking the gateway to heaven. In my fantasy, she's not wearing any panties and the smell of her musk is almost overwhelming. I nuzzle her with my nose and lips, biting her gently on the leg, enjoying the shudders that run through her. I explore all of her as I lick and tease and probe her with my tongue and fingers.

She would take my head in her hands, running those pink digits through my curly hair as she starts to rock back and forth, driving into me harder and harder. Now I'm sucking as hard as I can, swaying with her, barely able to breathe, but unable to stop; thrusting until we plunge over the edge of the cliff of pleasure and she closes around me like an oyster around a pearl.

I'm done for the day, ready to go home and touch myself, thinking about today's session, when she brings me out of my reverie.

"I've noticed you're breathing faster, are you feeling anxious today?" She's smiling at me, her lips full and inviting.

"No," I say. "I feel really good today." I stretch, my arms behind my back, thrusting out my little bud breasts, hoping she'll notice I've left an extra button on the flannel undone.

"Good. I think you've made great progress. Maybe we should think about you finishing up your course of therapy?"

My heart starts pounding in my chest and I feel nauseous. Never see her again? Miss my weekly fantasy? "No," I say too quickly. "I'm not doing as well as you think. There's something I haven't been telling you."

"Oh," she says, licking her lips nervously. "Well, then, I'll see you next week. Same time?"

Relieved, I nod. "Next week," I agree. I'm sure I can think up a good problem by next week.

First Water, Then Light

Suki Lee

It was the memory of Sara that came to me first, even though it was Rachel and the wine I'd just ordered that I was waiting for. The apparition of Sara's curls, close-cropped to her head, shimmered dragon-like. Her imagined laughter rose above clinking glasses. But it was Rachel's lateness for our first date that propelled me to leave the café, in search of Sara.

I decided I would tell Rachel I was off to the bank machine if our paths crossed. I hurried, Sara-bound, an obsessive somnambulist. I don't actually consider myself compulsive, yet mere minutes later, I was standing below Sara's apartment window. Nasturtiums swayed in their boxes above, which brought to mind her love affair with plants. Throughout our three years together, Sara would spring out of bed, leaving my hands reaching for the touch of her bronze skin. I'd hear her naked feet pad across the floor to the balcony, then the sound of water pouring over flowers. Alone in our bed, I always imagined Sara's nipples hardening in the brisk morning air beneath the embrace of her thin cotton wrap. Her voice would float back to me as she adoringly called them her pets, her loves. Some would think it strange that I was envious of flowers.

I slipped into the building after the front door was held open for me. Once inside, my feet followed a familiar path to Sara's apartment. I ran my fingers along the stairwell, pretending that it was really down the delicate skin of Sara's neck and along her clavicle, down to her breasts and along to her nipples, down and along the line of her.

What would I say when she opened the door?

"Sara, I've come to you even though there's a beautiful woman waiting for me at our favourite café."?

I walked up the stairs to the first floor into a small hallway that contained four closed apartment doors. It was the same hallway where Sara and I had our last failed kiss. Truth be told, our passion had exhausted itself after the first six months, but I'd held onto its memory.

All of a sudden, the door to my former home flew open. My heart leapt out of me and I caught it in a small alcove large enough for me to conceal myself, coffin-like. As I hid, I heard a long probing kiss, Sara's giggle, an unfamiliar woman's laughter, and footsteps down the stairs.

Throughout this, I was vaguely aware that my heartbeat was normal. I was quite calm. There were no feelings of loss, sadness, or much of anything other than the realization that I was an adult woman hiding in an alcove, spying on my former lover. I cradled myself in an embrace that was warmer than any Sara had given me in our last months together. What was I doing? It was over. I thought of Rachel. I should have been chasing my future, not my past.

As I came out of the alcove, a flat eyebrow looked back at me beside a round astounded mouth. It was the number 10 on our old apartment door, but I saw it more as my questioning conscience.

I found my way onto the street, walking back to the café where my wine – and hopefully Rachel – were waiting. I decided I would bring her flowers as an apology, something exotic, orchids maybe.

Ahead of me, I spotted Sara, strolling with her new girlfriend. There was a bounce to Sara's step that I hadn't seen for a long time. It actually made me happy for her. She'd never been like that with me. It was nice that she found what we'd been missing.

Before I knew it, I was walking right behind Sara and her new amour. I could see that Sara needed another dye job – her roots were showing. I had a ready smile and a friendly greeting in waiting if she turned around.

But it was her new partner who turned for an instant.

Her eyes widened at the sight of me.

I flushed as I returned her gaze. *Caught.* She obviously thought I was following them. Sara must have shown her my picture.

She looked me over.

There wasn't any recognition.

She smiled coquettishly.

Was she flirting with me?

I came to a full stop. Sara and this new girl moved on.

I watched them go. It was merely a protective impulse. I didn't want this woman to break Sara's heart.

I walked on to the café, hoping Rachel was still waiting. What I didn't realize immediately is that the end of the scenario had played itself out adjacent to our rendezvous point. Rachel had been watching me the entire time.

"Friends?" Rachel questioned.

"Sort of," I said. I sat before my wine and noticed she'd helped herself to a few sips. The red imprint of her lips covered the rim.

Rachel looked so deeply into me that truth came to the skin. When I looked back, her eyes calmed me with their blue. It was her, she was the one I'd been searching for all along.

A Real Life Superhero

Kate Dominic

I want to be Xena.

Actually, I don't want to be *Xena*. Maintaining a body like hers would be way too much work. I want to be a strong, sexy, all-muscle-no-fat warrior woman with royal connections – someone everybody knows will save the world, every time.

I want to be a real life superhero – Jeena.

My sidekick will be Arielle. She has long blonde hair and is very feminine – voluptuous, even – in a muscular, superhero sidekick-ish sort of way. She's good with swords, a worthy companion, someone I can always trust to protect my back and fight at my side. We're totally in love, of course, touching each other whenever we want. Nobody minds. After all, we're superheroes and can do no wrong.

In one adventure, Arielle and I are perusing a stand of ripe fruit in a typical open marketplace in a typical medieval village. I run my hands along the smooth, bare flesh below the short silk top that struggles to contain my lover's breasts. As I'm looking at the apples, I lift her skirt and caress the curve of her luscious bottom. The villagers laugh encouragingly when I slip my fingers into Arielle's slick folds and draw out fingers dripping with her sex honey. I bark an order at the baker. She hands me a loaf of hot, fresh bread. I smear the sticky juices on it. I take a bite, then share it with Arielle. She licks my fingers appreciatively, spreading her legs wide for me to prepare another slice.

The women in the village nod knowingly at each other. "*That's* the way you're supposed to do things. Like Jeena does!" they say. There's a rush on the baker's cart, followed by the rustle of more skirts being lifted and the contented moans of women being fingered. Then the sounds of people chewing as everybody has a mid-afternoon snack. Afternoon snack becomes a new tradition in the village – and they prosper forever after because everyone is so happy and energized.

In another of my favorite adventures, I teach the local nobility the proper way to negotiate a peace treaty. The meeting takes place in the castle of one of the feuding overlords. The combatants are a mixed crowd, some women, some men, all highly impressed with their titles and armies.

As I enter the room, the assemblage rises from their seats at the great table – the women aloof in their satin dresses and silken veils, the men prim and proper in their velvet clothes. There's a collective gasp as I saunter over to my chair – wearing nothing but my boots, weapon harnesses, and my jewelry. Arielle walks at my side – barefoot, shoulders erect, naked. As I sit down, Arielle kneels beside me, resting her staff against the back of the chair. She licks my breasts, and I start to speak.

"We'll get nothing accomplished if our minds stay focused on anger and differences. Everyone remove your clothing and get comfortable. That will put us all on equal footing." I shiver as Arielle licks a particularly delicious spot. "Then we're going to settle this matter once and for all. Strip!"

No one resists Jeena's orders. Veils and shifts and tunics drop to the floor. An army of servants appears to salvage the clothing.

"A properly negotiated treaty will be in everyone's best interests." As I speak, I let them see how much Arielle's ministrations turn me on. My nipples are hard and erect, glistening with my lover's saliva. Arielle moves between my legs, licking her way downward. There's a loud murmur of stunned disbelief. When her hot, probing tongue slides between my labia, I hold up my hand for silence.

"Excuse me," I say, letting my voice quiver with pleasure. "My side-kick's tongue is quite delicious. I must indulge myself before I can concentrate on business." With that, I slide further down in the chair.

I shudder visibly, then take a deep breath, looking pointedly around. "I said get comfortable!" I rest my hand on the back of Arielle's head. "If you need pointers, watch Arielle. Pay particular attention to how she's sucking my clit while she fingers her own." With that, I close my eyes and lift my boots up to rest against the edge of the table.

I watch from the corners of my eyes as shocked murmurs give rise to appraising glances. One of the overladies leans back in her chair, followed by another. Pretty soon all the former combatants are comfortably ensconced, their seconds-in-command between their legs, studiously following Arielle's sterling example. Before long, the hot smells of good sex and the general sound of contented slurping fill the room. I close my eyes all the way and enjoy as Arielle's hot tongue teases an orgasm from me.

When my breath settles, I speak again, motioning those who haven't yet climaxed to continue and participate as they're ready. "This is how we're going to do business."

The conference lasts all day. I don't keep track of the number of times I climax. Sometimes I lift Arielle onto the table in front of me so I can bury my face in the honeyed feast between her legs. Later on, I eat my lunch off her belly, feeding her with my fingers as I address yet another point in the negotiations. I savor her pussy, then give her mine for dessert. As the negotiations draw to a close, I lift Arielle to her feet and kiss her soundly. She picks up her staff and stands behind me – sturdy, proud, her face glistening with my juices and flushed from her many climaxes. She blushes even deeper as the sated negotiators thank her with a round of thunderous applause. She's every bit a true superhero sidekick, and together, we've once more saved the day.

motorcycle confusion

lisa g

I shouldn't have bought the motorcycle. Let's get that out of the way, *right* away. What I was really doing was checking *him* out, not the bike. I felt a stirring that was disconcerting. Let's face it, I felt confused.

The whole thing started when I called the phone number from a hand-drawn cardboard sign. I'd been half-heartedly looking for a motorcycle for about four months; want ads, used bike shops, but it was such a macho club, this world of motorcycles, and frankly the thought of handing over some money to a guy who was looking down his nose at me made me crazy. You see, before that my girlfriend had dumped me and my ego was broken. I needed to make serious changes. I decided that learning some practical mechanical skills, donning a leather outfit, and placing a big engine between my thighs would be the perfect remedy. So I made an appointment with the surprisingly charming voice over the phone and went over to check it out. The owner was all proud and shy and plaid flannel, his shaggy blonde bangs falling over one eye. I trusted him immediately. The bike was all black and sleek and shiny. Compact with a decent engine: 400cc. It was well taken care of, only a smidgen of rust on the tailpipe. I wanted to straddle it right away. I felt giddy, then weird. Was this feeling really about finding the bike of my dreams? And the guy was so nice about it all. So unassuming. He didn't make me feel dumb. I asked questions I had been told to ask about the condition of the engine. I kicked the tires. We laughed together at our shared inexperience. He admitted he didn't know a lot about bikes but had been able to, you know, change the oil and grease the chain. He had ridden it down the coast of Oregon alone. He was so appealing that I kept asking questions so I could hang around. I ran my hand along the gas tank as we talked. I stroked the seat. I noticed the tachometer was busted so I fingered that too. We bent down together to admire the carbs. He had recently cleaned them. I pictured him rubbing the metal. His hands were so perfect. His mannerisms were delicate. He moved around the bike with such apology and his ass . . . oh. I asked if I could think about it. The bike that is. I was woozy pedaling my bicycle back home and I just couldn't figure it out. I lay on my back porch in the sun looking up into the blue sky and wispy white clouds. I felt almost at peace. You just love who you love – that's all. Neither boy nor girl should matter. But I faltered. My mind raced. I couldn't help it.

Cock.

There I said it. Not a latex facsimile. A real human tube of flesh. I tried to imagine sucking his cock. Why did I always have to take it there? Couldn't I just be his friend? Couldn't I just love him as a friend? Nothing made sense to me. I called him back immediately and asked if we could get together – to get the bike looked at – in the shop by my house. All I wanted was to be near him and the only way I knew how was to pretend to buy his motorcycle. His voice over the phone made a bee line to my crotch. I couldn't deny it.

The next day we met at the shop to have the bike checked out. The man behind the counter said it would take two hours. Two hours! Without hesitation I said, "Should we go for coffee?"

Caffeine was the last thing I needed since my heart was already pounding a mile a minute, but hell, he accepted. We sat in a tan pleather booth and his eyes lit up as he recalled camping trips using a tarp attached to his handlebars like a tent. I wondered if the tarp was as blue as his eyes, then I feared I was obviously mooning. Hanging on his every word I became a pathetic straight teenager. Then he told me he was moving to Europe to be with his *girlfriend*.

The bike checked out with flying colors, and was worth $500 more than he was charging. So I took it for a spin. I didn't feel at all judged as I swerved under the weight. It felt good enough, I guess. I had ridden a few different makes and models and it handled better than the Harley and worse than the dirt bike. I convinced myself that I needed it. Did buying his bike signify a bond for us to share for eternity? I told myself that I wanted to help him. I wanted him to be happy. What I wasn't admitting to was that I wanted to hold him and kiss him and . . . but he had a girlfriend and I was queer, so instead, I told him I would buy his bike. I had a few more fantasy-filled days of contact with him: papers to sign, rain gear to throw in, a few voice mail messages telling me intimate things I should know about the starter and the right turn signal. I kept his gravelly voice on my machine long after he had left for Europe.

The world is small, of course, and it was through mutual friends that I found out more about this fabulous stranger. He was once a *she*. Well, that sure explained his allure. I will not deny I felt a sense of relief. I do relish my queer standing. And although I still didn't know the status of his "cock" per se – I no longer cared – since there is nothing I find more sexy than the person strong enough to be who they are, at any cost. I probably didn't necessarily need to buy the bike but nonetheless – *pleased to meet you, my motorcycle boyfriend. You are forever in my heart.*

It Takes a Village

Carol Demech

I have to thank my best friend Jo for getting me into this business. I can still remember the day that I met her at a women's consciousness-raising group in 1972. Back then I was straight, a flower child, young and innocent. Jo walked into the meeting and I melted. She looked like John Denver and I was in love. It lasted for three months. I realized I preferred women who looked more like Janis Joplin than John Denver. Jo and I remained friends and a year later she met Shelly. They have been together ever since.

Jo and Shelly live a more conservative lifestyle than Ozzie and Harriet. I don't want you to think they're boring. It's just that they're to the right of white bread. They live in suburbia, have a big house, a boat, a BMW, a motorcycle, and a large pick-up truck. Jo is a gym teacher who lives and breathes softball, which she coaches five evenings a week and all day Saturday. Shelly is a corporate vice-president who frequently works late. They are a typical, suburban upwardly mobile lesbian couple; they rarely see each other.

Not wanting to suffer from lesbian bed death, they have vanilla sex once a week whether they want to or not. Jo sometimes wishes Shelly were more creative in bed. Jo once asked Shelly about trying something different in the bedroom. Shelly thought it was a good idea and began to redecorate. Jo thought that maybe they could try sex toys. One afternoon at my house, Jo asked me to show her my toys. I took my favorite out of my toy drawer. Jo gasped at its size and her color changed to a deep maroon. She turned away and muttered, Shelly would never, could never, my God that's big!

One night Jo tried wearing nothing but cologne to bed and suggested to Shelly that she sleep in something a bit more suggestive or provocative than flannel pajamas and socks, which she wore to bed because she was always cold. Another night, she tried something kinky. Jo wore one of her ties to bed but Shelly said it was getting in her way. Shelly wouldn't do anything that would break a nail or mess up her hair.

Jo then decided that she wanted a baby. They were both in their late forties and Jo thought having a baby might spice up their life. Spice, more like reliving your childhood with less control than you had with your own. Get a pet, I begged, but Jo was determined to become a mother.

Shelly reluctantly agreed after Jo convinced her that their lives wouldn't change much, only the diapers would. Five trips to the fertility clinic in New York proved fruitless. Jo had a limited number of eggs and they were, according to the doctor, slow and not likely to fertilize. (The eggs seemed pretty smart to me.) Jo needed eggs, but Shelly had had a hysterectomy. Don't ask me, "I'm in menopause, no eggs here."

They considered adoption, but Jo insisted on having her own. So they decided to find donated eggs and donated sperm. They wanted to know what they were getting, so they did comparative shopping. They finally settled for sperm from a sperm bank in New Jersey and eggs from a fertility clinic in New York City. The prices were good and locally produced, so to speak. Shelly, always thinking of maximizing profits and saving money, was especially happy that there would be no shipping costs and unnecessary wear and tear.

The New Jersey bank told them that the sperm was from a handsome medical student with a lifeguard's body. The eggs were from a sophisticated, gorgeous young attorney who graduated from Columbia University. The perfect couple. I told Jo not to ask for my opinion, but she did. Being the cynic that I am, my first thought was that the sperm was from some enterprising young man who drifted from clinic to clinic watching free porn or a Mafioso who had helped bury Jimmy Hoffa under the fifty yard line at the Giants Stadium in the Meadowlands.

It also didn't make sense to me that an attorney who was an Ivy League graduate with a six-figure salary would sell her eggs for a few thousand dollars. Of course, it made sense to Shelly, she imagined that the young woman was on a fast track to the top and not having time to do volunteer work, felt she could contribute to society by giving up a few hours of her life to donate her eggs. Shelly said it was like donating blood, same principle.

The sperm needed to be picked up in New Jersey and delivered to the fertility clinic in New York City where Jo would have the fertilized eggs implanted in her womb. On the day of the conception, Shelly was too busy to go so I was elected conception assistant. When we arrived at the bank, Jo asked if I could do one of those Goddess rituals to bless the sperm. Jo wanted to encourage the boy sperm to be aggressive when they were racing to fertilize the egg. She wanted a son to play ball with.

Shelly called to remind Jo to get receipts. All of the costs for having a baby were a tax write-off. Shelly also wanted a receipt from me, the sperm carrier. She was sure that there was a deduction for that. The sperm was packaged in a large styrofoam cooler. In the car, I placed the cooler on my lap and Jo reminded me to hold onto it for dear life.

So, there I was, a card-carrying dyke, holding on my lap a container of frozen sperm. The New Jersey Turnpike would never seem the same to me again. That's when I decided to go into business. I could deliver sperm to lesbian couples and eggs to gay men. No, the eggs wouldn't work. What would they do with them? Probably make a quiche or a fabulous Hollandaise sauce. I'd stick to sperm. The company would be called Dyke and Dyke Sperm – DADS. The sperm would come in dildos and every dyke could be both a mom and a dad.

Ten years later and DADS is doing a multi-million dollar business. We have a website and deliver sperm to lesbian couples all over the world. All of our sperm carriers are lesbians personally certified by me. DADS is a global company with offices in New York City, San Francisco, Paris, London, and Toronto. Within two years, we plan to open a DADS office in Buenos Aires and Bangkok.

Jo and Shelly have a wonderful son. Even though he doesn't like to play ball, Jo brags that he is just like Shelly, not wanting to break any of his nails that Shelly just polished. And that is how I started my business, Oprah.

Nomi's Phone Call

Karen X. Tulchinsky

I push open the apartment door to find my roommate Betty slumped in her usual spot, on the sofa – my bed – channel surfing. I try to sneak past her into the kitchen. We had a fight earlier. I'm not sure if we're getting along.

"Sit down, Nom," she says. "Look." She points at the TV screen with the remote control. "It's Ellen's coming out episode."

"I've seen it."

Betty gives me a look. "Yeah. But how many times?"

"Six or seven."

"That's all? What kind of a lesbian are you? Come on, sit down."

I plop onto the sofa. It's the scene where Ellen is in a hotel room with the scrawny guy, her old friend.

"Men, men, men," says Ellen. "Boy do I love men."

"You're not mad at me?" I ask Betty.

"Shit, girl. No. I thought you were mad at me."

"No."

"Good. Now shut up. I want to see this."

"Show me the money," says Ellen, pushing the guy onto the big double bed and pouncing on him.

"How many times have *you* seen this?" I ask.

"Shhhh," says Betty.

We watch the show. Ellen and the guy start making out. Then something goes wrong, and Ellen jumps up, and kicks the guy out into the hall. A commercial comes on.

"Oh. Almost forgot." Betty says. "Your girlfriend called."

I leap up. "Julie?"

"Who else?"

I dash into Betty's bedroom to use the phone in private.

"Hey!" she calls after me, "don't you wanna see the part where Ellen comes out?"

But I'm already dialing Julie's number.

"What are you wearing?" Julie asks in a sultry voice. I slip further down on the bed, stretch my legs out. This is what you do when you're in a long distance relationship. You have phone sex.

Just as I'm about to answer, the phone beeps. Call waiting. I hate call waiting, but it could be for Betty. She made me promise to always answer in case one of her many babes is trying to reach her. God forbid she misses a call. "Julie. Can you hold on for a second?"

"O-kay," she sounds annoyed. Who can blame her?

I flick the button down once. "Hello?"

"Hello, Nomi?"

It's my mother.

"Hi, Ma. Listen, I'm on the other line. Can I call you back later?"

"Sure, Nomi. I'm only your mother. Why talk to me?"

"Ma. Come on. Don't be like that."

"Who knows if I'll be here."

I'm not going to fall for my mother's tactics. "I'll call you back soon."

"Fine." She says this as if she is on death row, and her life is doomed.

I hit the phone button twice. "Julie?"

"I was just about to hang up. Who was it? Your other girlfriend?"

"My mother. Julie, you're my only girlfriend."

"Are you sure?"

"What do you think?"

"Then answer my question." she demands.

"Question?"

"What are you wearing?"

"Oh. Black leather chaps," I lie. "And a tight black tee." Really I'm wearing baggy blue jeans and a stained denim shirt.

"Ask me what I'm wearing?" she urges.

"What are you wearing," I glance at the bedroom door that unfortunately has no lock and hope like hell Ellen's coming out show is enthralling enough to keep Betty in the living room for a while.

"Black negligee," Julie answers. "Lace, with a low . . . low neckline. And Nomi. . . . "

"Yes." She is turning me on.

"No panties."

"Oh God." My hand finds its way between my legs. "Tell me more."

"I'm wet for you, Nomi."

The phone beeps. "Shit."

"Don't answer it, Nomi."

"Shit."

"Please, baby. . . ."

"Sorry. I promised Betty. She's expecting a call. Don't go away. Please, babe."

She sighs. "All right."

I push the button. "Hello!" I bark.

"Nomi . . . I'm waiting."

"Ma!" I shout, "what are you doing? I said I'd call you when I'm finished."

"I thought you forgot about me."

"I'm hanging up on you, Ma."

"Fine. I can see I'm not important enough."

"Goodbye, Ma." I hit the button. "Julie." There is silence but no dial tone. "Julie?"

"I'm here, Nomi."

"Where were we?"

"I was just slipping out of my negligee."

"Oh God. Where are you?"

"In the bedroom."

"Take it off slowly," I instruct. "And describe it to me."

"I'm slipping off the top part. . . ." Julie says. "My breasts are exposed. My nipples are hard."

I sink lower on Betty's bed, getting back in the mood. "Yes. . . ." I urge.

"I'm touching my nipples. Squeezing them."

"Julie. . . ." I undo the top button on my jeans.

The door swings open. Betty bursts in, the remote control clutched in her hand.

"You gotta see this, Nom. It's the best part, you know, where Ellen has a crush on Laura Dern."

"Betty!" I leap to my feet. "Can't you knock?"

"It is *my* room, Nomi." She is offended. "Oh." She understands. "Why didn't you tell me you were having phone sex? Hi Julie, how's it going?" she yells in the general direction of the phone receiver. She turns on her heels. "Well, I guess you couldn't care less about Ellen. Lucky for you I'm taping this." She closes the door behind her.

"Julie?" I say into the phone.

"Nomi, why don't you just call me tomorrow?" Her voice is tense.

"How about later?"

"It'll be too late here. I have to go to sleep."

"It's okay now. Betty won't come back."

"What about your mother?"

"I won't answer if it beeps again."

"What about the call Betty's waiting for?"

I sigh. Deeply.

"Goodbye, Nomi. Call me tomorrow."

"I love you," I say tentatively.

Her voice softens. "I love you too."

The second I hang up, the phone rings. I pick it up.

"Hello Ma."

"How did you know it was me?"

"Phychic I guess."

"Nomi! You're not involved in one of those psychedelic cults down there in California, are you?"

"Yeah, the cult of annoyed daughters."

"Are you?"

"Ma, it's not the sixties."

When she finally gets to it, her big emergency was whether or not to invite my Aunt Celia to the Passover Seder, because she had a falling out with her sister, Lydia. I offer my humble advice and hang up the phone, slip out of the bedroom and into the living room. Betty is sitting on the edge of her seat. Ellen is in an airport waiting room sitting beside Laura Dern. Then Ellen follows Laura into the passenger line up, and with the Flight Attendant's microphone an inch from her face, unbeknownst to her, Ellen tells the entire waiting room, "I'm gay."

Betty glances at me. "You go, girl," she tells Ellen.

Ellen realizes her blunder, turns three shades of red. Laura hugs her. The commercial break comes on. My eyes glaze over. All I can think about is Julie.

Out on Main Street

Shani Mootoo

Janet and me? We does go Main Street to see pretty pretty sari and bangle, and to eat we belly full a burfi and gulub jamoon, but we doh go too often because, yuh see, is dem sweets self what does give people like we a presupposition for untameable hip and thigh.

Another reason we shy to frequent dere is dat we is watered-down Indians – we ain't good grade A Indians. We skin brown, is true, but we doh even think 'bout India unless something happen over dere and it come on de news. Mih family remain Hindu ever since mih ancestors leave India behind, but nowadays dey doh believe in praying unless things real bad, because, as mih father always singing, like if is a mantra: "Do good and good will be bestowed unto you." So he is a veritable saint 'cause he always doing good by his women friends and dey chilren. I sure some a dem must be mih half sister and brother, oui!

Mostly, back home, we is kitchen Indians: some kind a Indian food every day, at least once a day, but we doh get cardamom and other fancy spice down dere so de food not spicy like Indian food I eat in restaurants up here. But it have one thing we doh make joke 'bout down dere: we like we meethai and sweetrice too much, and it remain overly authentic, like de day Naana and Naani step off de boat in Port of Spain harbor over a hundred and sixty years ago. Check out dese hips here nah, dey is pure sugar and condensed milk, pure sweetness!

But Janet family different. In de ole days when Canadian missionaries land in Trinidad dey used to make a bee-line straight for Indians from down South. And Janet great grandparents is one a de first South families dat exchange over from Indian to Presbyterian. Dat was a long time ago.

When Janet born, she father, one Mr John Mahase, insist on asking de Reverend MacDougal from Trace Settlement Church, a leftover from de Canadian Mission, to name de baby girl. De good Reverend choose de name Constance 'cause dat was his mother name. But de mother a de child, Mrs Savitri Mahase, wanted to name de child sheself. Ever since Savitri was a lil girl she like de yellow hair, fair skin, and pretty pretty clothes Janet and John used to wear in de primary school reader – since she lil she want to change her name from Savitri to Janet, but she own father get vex and say how Savitri was his mother name and how she will insult his mother if she gone and change it. So Savitri get she own way once by marrying this fella name John, and she do a encore, by calling her daughter Janet, even doh husband John upset for days at she for insulting de good Reverend by throwing out de name a de Reverend mother.

So dat is how my girlfriend, a darkskin Indian girl with thick black hair (pretty fuh so!) get a name like Janet.

She come from a long line a Presbyterian school teacher, headmaster and headmistress. Savitri still teaching from de same Janet and John reader in a primary school in San Fernando, and John, getting more and more obtuse in his ole age, is headmaster more dan twenty years now in Princes Town Boys' Presbyterian High School. Everybody back home know dat family good good. Dat is why Janet leave in two twos. Soon as A Level finish she pack up and take off like a jet plane so she could live without people only shoo-shooing behind she back. . . . "But A A! Yuh ain't hear de goods 'bout John Mahase daughter, gyul? How yuh mean yuh ain't hear? Is big thing! Everybody talking 'bout she. Hear dis, nah! Yuh ever see she wear a dress? Yes! Doh look at mih so. Yuh reading mih right!"

Is only recentish I realize Mahase is a Hindu last name. In de ole days every Mahase in de country turn Presbyterian and now de name doh have no association with Hindu or Indian whatsoever. I used to think of it as a Presbyterian Church name until some days ago when we meet a Hindu fella fresh from India name Yogdesh Mahase who never even hear of Presbyterian.

De other day I ask Janet what she know 'bout Divali. She say, "It's the Hindu festival of lights, isn't it?" like a line straight out a dictionary. Yuh think she know anything 'bout how lord Rama get himself exile in a forest for fourteen years, and how when it come time for him to go back home his followers light up a pathway to help him make his way out, and dat is what Divali lights is all about? All Janet know is 'bout going for drive in de country to see light, and she could remember looking forward, around Divali time, to the lil brown paper-bag packages full a burfi and parasad that she father Hindu students used to bring for him.

One time in a Indian restaurant she ask for parasad for dessert. Well! Since den I never go back in dat restaurant, I embarrass fuh so!

I used to think I was a Hindu *par excellence* until I come up here and see real flesh and blood Indian from India. Up here, I learning 'bout all kind a custom and food and music and clothes dat we never see or hear 'bout in good ole Trinidad. Is de next best thing to going to India, in truth, oui! But Indian store clerk on Main Street doh have no patience with us, specially when we talking English to dem. Yuh ask dem a question in English and dey insist on giving de answer in Hindi or Punjabi or Urdu or Gujarati. How I suppose to know de difference even! And den dey look at yuh disdainful – like yuh disloyal, like yuh is a traitor.

But yuh know, it have one other reason I real reluctant to go Main Street. Yuh see, Janet pretty fuh so! And I doh like de way men does look at she, as if because she wearing jeans and T-shirt and high-heel shoe and make-up and have long hair loose and flying about like she is a walking-talking shampoo ad, dat she easy. And de women always looking at she beady eye, like she loose and going to thief dey man. Dat kind of thing always make me want to put mih arm round she waist like, she is my woman, take yuh eyes off she! and shock de false teeth right out dey mouth. And den is a whole other story when dey see me with mih crew cut and mih blue jeans tuck inside mih jim-boots. Walking next to Janet, who so femme dat she redundant, tend to make me look like a gender dey forget to classify. Before going Main Street I does parade in front de mirror practicing a jiggly-wiggly kind a walk. But if I ain't walking like a strong-man monkey I doh exactly feel right and I always revert back to mih true colors. De men dem does look at me like if dey is exactly what I need a taste of to cure me good and proper. I could see dey eyes watching Janet and me, dey face growing dark as dey imagining all kind a situation and position. And de women dem embarrass fuh so to watch me in mih eye, like dey fraid I will jump up and try to kiss dem, or make pass at dem. Yuh know, sometimes I wonder if I ain't mad enough to do it just for a little bacchanal, nah!

Going for a outing with mih Janet on Main Street ain't easy! If only it wasn't for burfi and gulub jamoon. If only I had a learned how to cook dem kind of thing before I leave home and come up here to live.

Notes on Contributors

DONNA ALLEGRA's collection of stories, *Witness to the League of Blond Hip Hop Dancers*, was published by Alyson. Her poetry and essays are published in anthologies that include *Home Girls, Hers: Brilliant New Fiction by Lesbians* (1 and 3), *Does Your Mama Know? An Anthology of Black Lesbian Coming-Out Stories*, and *Hot & Bothered: Short Short Fiction on Lesbian Desire* (1, 2, and 3).

WENDY ATKIN lives and works in Ottawa, Ontario. Her story was written in the sunny spring snow at Moonstone, and she thanks Beth Mairs and her mother for this well-treed space.

Sex inspires LEAH BAROQUE to write, and writing inspires her to fuck. Her writing has been published in *Australian Women's Forum, Eroticus, Hot & Bothered 3, Libida, Paddles, Penthouse Variations, Scarlet Letters*, and *Wicked Words 5*. She looks forward to exploring both passions for a very long time!

DEGAN BELEY is a working writer and computer geek living in Vancouver. She enjoys writing erotica and short stories and is currently working on a novel entitled *The Most Passionate Girl*. "Pomegranate" is her first published story.

J.L. BELROSE's fiction appears in *Queer View Mirror, Pillow Talk II, Skin Deep I, Best Women's Erotica I, Uniform Sex, Set in Stone, Body Check*, and *Hot & Bothered 3*, as well as various magazines and journals. She wants to thank the women who inspire her to write.

SHARI J. BERMAN is a writer, translator, and entrepreneur. Her first novel, *Kona Dreams*, was released in English in 2002 and her serial, *The Selena Stories*, is online at *justicehouse.com*. The German editions of her first two novels are published by el!es. Other short fiction appears in publications from Alyson, Arsenal Pulp, el!es, and Robinson Publishing in the U.S., Canada, Germany, and the U.K.

CLAUDIA BERTY is originally from New York, but moved to a Great Northern City in Yorkshire, England, where she lives with her talented partner, Susannah, her three children, and two dogs. When not working as a doctor, she also sculpts, writes, and dances to '80s New Wave music.

BARRIE JEAN BORICH is the author of *My Lesbian Husband* (Graywolf Press), winner of an American Library Association GLBT book award. She lives with her beloved, Linnea Stenson, and their dogs, Dusty Springfield and Rosemary Clooney, in Minneapolis, Minnesota. Visit her website at *barriejeanborich.net*.

MICHELLE BOUCHÉ is a writer, teacher, consultant, and rabble rouser. Her erotica has been published in *Best Women's Erotica 2001*, *Myths Fantastic*, and in an upcoming issue of *Moist*. Thanks to Leslie and Eric for your help with this one.

BARBARA BROWN is a Toronto-based writer, artist, and psychotherapist whose work has been published in various anthologies and journals, including *Hot & Bothered 3*. She is editor of *My Breasts, My Choice: Journeys Through Surgery*, an exhibit and book exploring people's experience of breast and chest surgery through photography and storytelling.

GIOVANNA (JANET) CAPONE is a San Francisco Bay Area poet, fiction writer, editor, and playwright. Her work has appeared in numerous books, and she co-edited *Hey Paesan! Writing by Lesbians & Gay Men of Italian Descent* with Tommi Avicolli Mecca and Denise Nico Leto. Giovanna works in a library and teaches poetry workshops to children through California Poets in the Schools.

MIRIAM CARROLL is a chronologically gifted writer, artiste, volunteer worker, and is expecting her first great grand-daughter with much elation. She lives in Atlanta, Georgia with her partner of twelve years, and their pussycat.

CONNIE CHAPMAN writes fiction and creative non-fiction. She has published in *Hot and Bothered 2* and *3*, *Victoria Rainbow News*, and several academic journals. She lives on Vancouver Island and works in Vancouver.

VAUGHAN CHAPMAN writes in Surrey, B.C., has minimal hiking experience, and has had short fiction published in *Pottersfield Portfolio* and *The New Orphic Review*.

RITZ CHOW's words have appeared in Canadian feminist and poetry journals, and various anthologies including *Swallowing Clouds: An Anthology of Chinese-Canadian Poetry* and *Anti-Asian Violence in North America: Asian American and Asian Canadian Reflections on Hate, Healing, and Resistance*.

NINA D. writes, dances, and plays in lush Vancouver, B.C. She gives thanks for the abundance in this life.

MARY DAVIES grew up in Halifax, Nova Scotia. Her work has appeared in *Field*, *Common Lives/Lesbian Lives*, on *ScarletLetters.com*, and she writes a regular column for *ButchDykeBoy.com* called "Notes From a Comfortable Shoes Femme." She lives in Boston and is working on a novel.

TANYA DAVIS was born and raised on Prince Edward Island and now lives in Vancouver. She has performed spoken word poetry around town and is working towards a career in music, wherein she can combine her love of words and rhythm. She wrote her first novel when she was fourteen. It can be found at her parents' house in Prince Edward Island.

For the first fifty years of her life, LYN DAVIS was a U.S. resident who spent her days working behind someone else's desk and her nights writing short fiction and poetry. Now she lives in Victoria, B.C. where she is self-employed and can write any time she pleases.

NOTES ON CONTRIBUTORS

MARIA DE LOS RIOS, born in Cuba and raised in Venezuela, is a writer, poet, and storyteller. Published in *Revista Mujeres, Conmocion, Hot and Bothered 1* and *3, Tongues on Fire,* and *New to North America.* Served as member of the editorial board of the Latina lesbian magazine *Conmocion.*

CAROL DEMECH writes stories to honor the women she meets. She is a well-traveled dyke who likes adventure and always returns to New York City and the people she loves. Her newest adventure took her to the South Bronx.

KATE DOMINIC is the author of *Any 2 People, Kissing* (Down There Press). Her erotic short stories have appeared in dozens of publications, including *Lip Service, Tough Girls,* and several volumes of *Best Lesbian Erotica* and *Best Women's Erotica.* She considers all her characters to be sexual superheroes.

NISA DONNELLY is the author of two novels, *The Bar Stories* (St Martin's Press; Lambda Award for Lesbian Fiction) and *The Love Songs of Phoenix Bay* (St Martin's Press), the editor of *Mom* (Alyson Publications; Lambda Award for Anthologies), and author of many short stories and essays.

JOLIE DU PRÉ's erotica has appeared on the Internet, including the Galleries of the Erotica Readers and Writers Association.

SARAH ELLEN lives with her partner of twelve years in Bristol, England. Besides enthusiastically pursuing her writing aspirations, she works part-time as a scrub nurse within the operating department of the local children's hospital. This is her first published work.

LISA G loves to tell stories. She appreciates Karen X. for giving her a reason to finish editing any of them. She enjoys the opportunity to revisit her desires, check in, and revise. This year, her desires change depending on what costume she is wearing.

GABRIELLE GLANCY's work has appeared in *The New Yorker, The Paris Review, The American Poetry Review, New American Writing*, and many other journals. Born and raised in New York City, she has taught writing in the Middle East and London, and now lives in San Francisco where she is on the faculty in the Graduate Creative Writing Program at the University of San Francisco.

SARA GRAEFE is an award-winning playwright, screenwriter, and fiction writer. Her plays – which include the queer-themed *Scribbles* and *Yellow on Thursdays* – have been produced as far afield as Canada's National Arts Centre, Yukon's Nakai Theatre, the Edinburgh Festival Fringe, and the Sydney Opera House. She lives and loves in Vancouver.

FLORENCE GRANDVIEW has been amassing her memoirs in fits and starts over the past four decades. They have appeared previously in *Geist, The New Orphic Review,* and *Hot & Bothered 2* and *3*.

TERRIE HAMAZAKI has performed original work at the Fringe and Women in View Performing Arts Festivals. Her short story "Im'potence" was recently published in *The Fed Anthology* (Anvil Press). She currently seeks a loving home for her first novel.

McKINLEY M. HELLENES lives anywhere there is room. She often rides her bike across the city at 2 a.m., and when she gets home her cats are waiting for her. She has a pair of shoes she's comfortable in. She writes because she has to.

CORRINA HODGSON is a graduate of the MFA programme in Creative Writing at the University of British Columbia. Her plays have been produced in Canada (Teatro Berdache, Buddies in Bad Times) and off-off Broadway. She currently freelances as a dramaturge at the National Theatre School while working toward her PHD at the University of Guelph.

NAIRNE HOLTZ's work has been published in various literary journals and anthologies since 2001. She has created a comprehensive annotated bibliography of Canadian lesbian and bisexual women's fiction that is available on the web. She lives in Montreal with her lesbian husband and miniature dogs.

ANH-THU HUYNH immigrated to Canada twenty years ago as a refugee from the political regime of the Communist Party of Vietnam. At thirteen, she was packed on a tiny boat crossing the ocean looking for freedom. She has led a life of a refugee, citizen without nation, child without parents, resident without home.

MELINDA JOHNSTON is a Vancouver writer who has been published in *emerge*, *Xtra! West*, and *Outlooks*. She usually writes stories that she can't show to her mother, and is currently working on a cycle of stories about women, sex, and violence.

SHANNON KIZZIA, a retired professional ballet dancer from Oklahoma, is twenty-nine and now lives in Mount Shasta, California. She's in a polyamorous relationship with two loving partners, Satina and David, and is proud to be helping to raise their two children.

TAMAI KOBAYASHI was born in Japan and raised in Canada. She is the author of *All Names Spoken* (co-authored with Mona Oikawa, Sister Vision Press), *Exile and the Heart* (Women's Press), and *Quixotic Erotic* (Arsenal Pulp), and is also a film and videomaker, screenwriter, and songwriter. She lives in Toronto.

SUKI LEE is an Ottawa writer whose fiction has been published in numerous literary journals, as well as *Hot & Bothered 3*. She writes the column "Sapphic Traffic" for *Capital Xtra!*, Ottawa's gay and lesbian monthly. Her collection of short stories, also entitled *Sapphic Traffic*, is being published in 2003.

ANYA LEVIN is a writer who finds exploring a fictional character's sexual life easier than trying to manage her own real-life relationship. Difficulty aside, she and her partner have been together for six years. Anya lives with said partner in the suburbs of Philadelphia, Pennsylvania.

JUDY LIGHTWATER is a writer, non-profit management consultant, and activist living in Victoria, B.C. Her fiction and humor writing have recently been published in *Prairie Fire* and *Monday Magazine*. "Oceans, Lakes, and Ice Cream" is an excerpt from a novel-in-progress entitled *The Women of Bertha Bay*.

N.M. MARO holds a BA in English from Wells College. Her work has appeared in *The Healing Muse* and Incarnate Muse Press's anthology *Above Us Only Sky*. She is a graduate student at Binghamton University and resides with her partner (not a Beckie[y]) in Ithaca, New York.

ELAINA MARTIN is an Ottawa singer/songwriter who released an independent CD *Cancer Woman* in 2002. Elaina has also produced and directed some of the most successful music and women's events in the Ottawa area. This is the first story she's written.

L.M. MCARTHUR works and lives in the Vancouver area with her partner of eight years and their cat Cali. She was previously published in *Hot & Bothered* 2 and 3.

GABRIEL MCCORMACK is currently studying film and graphic design in Vancouver. "What Might Have Been" is her first published piece. Her hobbies include leg wrestling, karaoke, and trivia board games. Adrenaline-rush sports also keep her busy between her travels and artistic pursuits.

MARY MIDGETT (AKA MIDGETT) resides in San Francisco, writes short stories, and is the author of *Brown on Brown, Black Lesbian Erotica*. She is a contributor to seven anthologies, three of which are *Hot and Bothered*. Her book *Cinnamon on Toast* will be released on her website this winter.

ANDREA MILLER, from Halifax, Nova Scotia, is currently living in Mexico. A certified yoga teacher, she has degrees in journalism and English literature. Her writing also appears in *Best Lesbian Erotica 2004*.

SHANI MOOTOO was born in Ireland and grew up in Trinidad. She is the author of the short fiction collection *Out on Main Street* and a novel *Cereus Blooms at Night*, which was shortlisted for the Chapters First Novel Award and the Giller Prize. She is also the author of a book of poetry *The Predicament of Or*. She lives in Vancouver.

LESLÉA NEWMAN has published over forty books, including *Girls Will Be Girls; She Loves Me, She Loves Me Not; Heather Has Two Mommies;* and *The Best Short Stories of Lesléa Newman*. Two new children's books, *The Boy Who Cried Fabulous* and *A Fire Engine for Ruthie* will be published in 2004. Visit *lesleanewman.com* to learn more about her work.

DENISE NICO LETO is a poet and editor living in the San Francisco Bay Area. Her poems and reviews have recently appeared in *Appetite: Food as Metaphor: An Anthology of Women Poets* from BOA, *Xantippe*, and *MELUS*.

CAROLYN NORBERG makes soup for a small coffee shop. Her first published story recently appeared in the *The Malahat Review*. She lives in Newfoundland.

JOY PARKS writes articles, interviews, and book reviews for many GLBT and mainstream magazines and newspapers. "Sacred Ground," her monthly column on lesbian writing, can be found online and in several lesbian publications. An award-winning advertising copywriter, Joy owns a creative consulting company and makes her home in Ottawa, Canada.

SYBIL PLANK lives in Ottawa, Canada.

CAROL QUEEN is an award-winning author of stories and essays about sex. She is the director of The Center for Sex & Culture, a non-profit educational organization in San Francisco, and works as staff sexologist at Good Vibrations. For more info visit *carolqueen.com*.

JANNIT RABINOVITCH is a lesbian-feminist mother of two teenagers who works with prostitutes and was appointed by the Attorney General to sit on the Victoria (B.C.) Police Board. She is currently doing her doctorate in Community Studies at the Union Institute and University. This is her first published piece of creative writing.

BETHIA RAYNE has worked as an English teacher in various countries including Finland and Borneo. She is a volunteer worker and counselor for LGBT in the U.K. and U.S. and has contributed to works on poverty and social exclusion within the gay community. She is currently studying for her Masters in Librarianship.

ELIZABETH ROUE lives quietly in Kamloops, B.C. with companions both two- and four-legged. Place doesn't matter much, as she lives mainly in her head. A variety of her poetry has been published on several websites, as well as book reviews for lesbian and academic publications, and a novel is in progress.

BRONWYN SCANLON is a writer, educator, and community project facilitator. She resides in a small studio apartment in St Kilda, Australia. Her short fiction and poetry have appeared in many anthologies and journals. Currently, she is completing her first novel entitled *Anything That Moves*.

STEPHANIE SCHROEDER is an interesting combination of chronic asthmatic breathlessness, compulsive Tourettic monloguing, and controlled hypo manic energy. Not your av-er-age Virgo, Stephanie is a proud pushy broad who lives and writes with her lover and muse, Tina, and their two pooches, Bacchus and Meka, in Brooklyn, New York.

ELFIE SCHUMACHER lives and works in Toronto. Her interests include lifting heavy objects high above her head, smoking, and hanging back meat curtains. "Transit" is based on her bus rides with the drummer for the Skinjobs.

HELENA SETTIMANA lives in Toronto. Her short fiction appears in diverse web and print publications in the U.S. and the U.K., including *Best Women's Erotica* series and *Mammoth Book of Best New Erotica Volume 2*. She is features editor at the Erotica Readers and Writers Association: *erotica-readers.com*.

WICKIE STAMPS has work in numerous anthologies including *Flashpoint, Close Calls, Queer View Mirror, Sons of Darkness*, and *Strategic Sex*. Wickie is a former editor of *Drummer* magazine and the lead writer on the award-winning short film *Foucault Who?*, a creepy crime drama.

MAR STEVENS is an afrocentric Libra living in Oakland, California. She writes to soothe her soul and those of others. She also writes to keep her lover Sandy, "hot and bothered." Her other passion is playing the African drums. She has been published in *Arise Magazine* and *Hot & Bothered 3*.

TAWANNA SULLIVAN lives in New Jersey with her life partner. She is the webmaster for Kuma – *kuma2.net* – a website which encourages black lesbians to write and share erotica.

SARAH B. WISEMAN currently lives in St John's, Newfoundland. Her erotica has appeared in *Hot And Bothered 3, Faster Pussycats*, and *Body Check*. She is also a poet and a carpenter.

MILJENKA ZADRAVEC is a Croatian lesbian. Her passions include social justice issues, animal rights, and the liberation of the body. She lives with her Doberman, Sammy. She is blessed with loving friends who inspire her writing and her heart. "Lavender Shoes" is an excerpt from her novel, which is still in progress.

About the Editor

Karen X. Tulchinsky is the award-winning author of *Love Ruins Everything*, named one of the Top Ten Books of 1998 by the *Bay Area Reporter*, its sequel, *Love and Other Ruins*; and *In Her Nature*, which won the VanCity Book Prize. Her most recent novel, *The Five Books of Moses Lapinsky*, was recently released. She is a graduate of the prestigious Canadian Film Centre, is a recipient of a B.C. Film Screenwriter's Fellowship, and has written for episodic television. She is the editor of numerous anthologies, including the best-selling *Hot & Bothered* series, the critically acclaimed *Queer View Mirror*, and the Lambda Literary Award finalist, *To Be Continued*. She has written for magazines and newspapers and teaches creative writing workshops and makes her home in Vancouver. Check out Karen's website at *karenxtulchinsky.com*

Photo: Daniel Collins